She's his lucky charm.
He's her biggest gamble.

Lucky Bet

REBECCA BARTO

For Joel,
My first and only love story

"Depend on the rabbit's foot if you will, but remember, it didn't work for the rabbit." —R.E. Shay

PROLOGUE

"If you still believe in fairness, then you've led a very lucky life."
—Leigh Bardugo

Rue hated the casino. The carpet underneath the roulette table smelled gross, and she was tired of playing on her mom's phone. she fell asleep, drifting off to the chimes from the slot machines, but her best friend came home from summer camp today, and Rue wanted to be chasing the ice cream truck or playing in the hydrant instead of being in stupid Atlantic City doing nothing again.

Well, not exactly nothing.

Rue sat criss-cross applesauce next to Momma's chair, picked at the strings of her denim shorts, and watched the legs of the adults. There were fat legs and hairy ones. Some wore fancy suit pants, while others poked out from mini skirts. Momma's legs were smooth and crossed demurely at the ankles, as if she were at synagogue instead of the casino.

After a while, her stomach rumbled, and she crawled out from under the table, reaching up to touch her mom's elbow.

"Momma?" She tried to keep the whining out of her voice. Momma hated whining. "I'm hungry."

Her mom flicked her cigarette into the glass ashtray balanced on the table rim, but didn't look down. The bangles on her wrist jangled as her free hand fell on the back of Rue's neck.

Rue winced. From a distance, the hand might have looked like a mother's loving touch, but underneath her dark hair, there were finger-shaped bruises from being rubbed like a genie lamp.

"Just one more minute, baby," her mom said, blowing smoke toward the ceiling. "And then we'll go to the buffet for some breakfast."

She'd said the same an hour ago. Rue didn't have a watch, but she could tell by the number of people milling around the casino floor that it was already early afternoon.

"Come up here and hold your Mama's hand," her mom said, patting Rue's head.

Rue stood up reluctantly, resting her chin on the table next to the ashtray. She wrinkled her nose at the stinky smell.

The dealer, a tired girl wearing a sparkly vest and a frown, didn't blink at the appearance of a six-year-old from under her roulette table.

Her mom gestured at the wheel with her cigarette, one heavy hand still gripping Rue's nape. "What should I pick, baby? 24, for your birthday? 30, for mine?"

Rue ignored the silly suggestion and studied the roulette wheel. Luck had nothing to do with birthdays or social security numbers, and they both knew it.

There was a time when she'd loved the casino. She'd love the lights and the noise and knowing exactly which number to pick to make her mom happy. Loved being swept into a hug and stopping for ice cream on the way home as a reward. Now the taste of mint chocolate chip made her sick.

Winning was a disease as sure as the sniffles or a fever. It crept behind the eyes and infected the heart. Even a first grader was smart enough to know what bad looked like.

"Well?" her mom said, taking another drag of her cigarette and nudging her with an elbow.

"What's it gonna be, Ace?" the dealer asked, one hand on the wheel and pity on her face. Her name was Aimee, and she was going to be a pharmacy tech and move to California as soon as she could make enough damn money to get out of this place.

Rue wasn't exactly sure why she should be ashamed to know that, just that she should.

She stood on her tiptoe to get a better look at the board. It was a regular roulette wheel. Anyone else who looked would see the wear along the edges where the dealer's hand spun or the smattering of broken pins. Only she could see the slight shimmer above the 18 like the heat on a sidewalk. Only she knew that it would be warmer than it should be if she touched it, as if the 18 had a fever.

Rue considered lying about what she saw, but only for a moment. Being good luck was what helped Mamma love her. She pointed.

"You sure, kiddo?" her mom asked, squinting at the number.

Rue gave her mom a look. She'd never been wrong.

They'd started noticing she was Lucky when her mom accidentally topped the national charts of an online poker game after only a few months of playing.

There were other signs too. Rue's kindergarten teacher had gotten pregnant after the baby doctor said she would never be a mommy. Mr. Macky, their next-door neighbor, stopped having tummy cancer even though the doctors said he would go to heaven. The bodega owner on the corner inherited millions of dollars from a distant relative, closed the shop, and moved to Florida.

The lottery tickets had been the clincher, though. Her mom hadn't worked since the day they'd lined up ten winning scratchers on the coffee table.

"Eighteen it is," Momma announced to the small gathering crowd of tourists, pushing her stack of chips onto the red square. Rue didn't know how to count, but it looked like a lot of money.

The dealer glanced up at the ceiling before accepting the bet, sliding it toward herself with the big stick.

Momma's hand twitched on the back of Rue's neck. They both knew what that glance meant. The big men in the ceiling didn't like them winning. It meant they were almost done for the day.

"Red, Eighteen," Aimee announced, reaching for the wheel.

The crowd watched as the roulette ball tinkered and bounced around the wheel, but Rue didn't have to look to know where it landed.

One

"Well, that isn't ideal," Rue muttered as the TV remote floated underneath the couch. She hesitated in the middle of her flooded living room, juggling an oversized bag of dog food and her work tote, as if someone was about to burst through the front door with a wrench and a hazelnut latte and make everything okay. Maybe a hunky boyfriend, or a best friend, or, at the very least, her deadbeat roommate.

There was no one, of course. Well, except Tugboat.

The three-year-old Great Dane observed her blandly from the top of the kitchen island, his massive paws crossed on a stack of junk mail, as if three inches of water were a routine occurrence in their shitty basement apartment.

"You've been home all day, and you didn't call me?" Rue scolded, sloshing over to the kitchenette.

Tug yawned in response. He weighed 130 pounds and was the laziest animal she'd ever met, but his gray fur was mottled with adorable black splatters, and he gave a pretty mean hug when she was weepy (which was bi-weekly at this point), so she let him stay with her rent-free.

The dog stretched as she heaved her bags beside him, his enormous, pink toebeans flashing. The movement knocked the pile of mail from the counter. It made a small splash in the water below.

"Nice," Rue grumbled.

Tug peered over the counter, long ears dangled as the mail sank into the floodwaters, but she didn't have time to rescue the bills because the kitchen faucet was running. Water splashed into the overflowing sink before cascading down the cabinet in a cheerful, burbling waterfall. Soap bubbles clung to the stainless steel and floated through the air.

"Shit!" Rue swore, kicking a floating bottle of Dawn as she lurched over to the sink and cut off the water. A stack of dirty dishes slid on the slick counter, and moisture clung to the cinderblock wall behind the sink.

Motherfucker.

"David," she yelled, trying to stay calm as she shoved up her sleeve and reached into the sink to pull the stopper. The arm of her coat dipped into the water anyway.

Rue couldn't remember the last time she'd seen her roommate. He bartended at a gay nightclub and only came home half the nights, but she'd seen his keys hanging on the hook by the door when she'd come in. The asshole was definitely here.

She called his name again, watching the sink water drain, and this time there was an answering thud from the back of the apartment, followed by a bleary curse.

"Coming!" David replied, his voice muffled by his closed bedroom door.

Rue kicked a bobbing Tupperware container with her toe before hoisting herself onto the island next to Tug. She toed off her ruined Converse, gritting her teeth at the little splash they made when they hit the water.

God, she was tired.

The Ikea mirror she'd bought to make the sad little living room look bigger leaned against the opposite wall, reflecting evidence of her current disaster. Through the steam, she caught a glimpse of a tired girl in a long wool coat (with one wet sleeve). Her thick brown hair wanted to frizz on a good day, but it had poofed impressively in the apartment's humidity. She looked like a damn tumbleweed.

Rue sighed, shrugging out of her wet coat. There had been a spay and neuter pop-up at work today, and there was a long scratch on her cheek from a particularly disgruntled tomcat.

It was a hazard of the job. She wouldn't trade it for the world.

She glanced in the mirror, noting the darkness underneath her usually bright green eyes. Okay, maybe *today* she would trade working at the shelter for a more relaxing job. Perhaps a massage therapist? Or one of those bookstore clerks?

Tug settled his big head on her thigh and sighed. Rue rubbed one soft ear between her thumb and finger, her throat tightening. Moisture dripped from the low popcorn ceiling. The unplayed guitar she bought on Marketplace last spring was filled with water, and the pile of dirty laundry she'd been meaning to take to the machines downstairs was soaked.

She was not going to cry.

It wasn't like crying wasn't a completely valid tool on a VERY BAD DAY, but it wasn't going to make her any drier.

This whole mess was her fault anyway—and by mess, she meant her entire life. It had been her decision to drop out of college after her first semester at NYU and buy a van and drive cross country, and then rent this grungy apartment with that shithead Aiden for two years before he accidentally fell in love with her neighbor and—

"Oh shit."

David sloshed into the living room wearing boxers and someone else's shirt—a sparkly lavender number that was at least two sizes too small. There was a mouth-shaped bruise on his neck and a club stamp on his hand. He was not alone.

The boy hovering behind him might have been the prettiest human Rue had ever seen, with striking blue eyes and the physique of one of those marble statues in Rome. They both surveyed the damage with a mixture of bewilderment and despair.

"David," Rue sighed, waving a hand at the now-empty kitchen sink.

Her roommate ran a hand through his bedhead, looking appropriately apologetic, just like he did the time he forgot to take out the trash for three weeks or when he brought home the cute blonde who turned out to be a kleptomaniac and stole both their laptops.

"Shit. I'm so sorry, babe; we must have gotten caught up..."
David trailed off, hand on his mouth. Rue didn't have to imagine
what they'd gotten caught up in—she'd walked in on him enough
times to have a horrifyingly accurate image.

"You left the water running," she said, as if it wasn't obvious.

"I'll call Mikey," he offered, hustling his date out the door with
a kiss on his perfect cheek.

"Oh, thank you so much," she said. She wasn't sure David even
knew where their landlord lived.

Tug took the moment to jump off the counter, knocking over a
lamp with his butt in the process. The bulb shatter-splashed when
it hit the water, but luckily, the movement yanked the wire out
of the wall before they were all electrocuted. The dog delicately
sniffed the floating shade.

David squelched back to the kitchen, still explaining how the
flood wasn't his fault (ADHD, apparently), and grabbed a protein
yogurt from their almost empty fridge. She was too tired to be mad
at either of them.

"He seems a little young for you," Rue said, watching a mouse
tread water beside the soggy basket of yarn beside the couch. She
kept meaning to learn to knit. Now it was too late.

"Bitch, he's the same age as me," David scoffed, peeling off the
top of his yogurt and licking it as if he wasn't standing up to his
ankles in water.

"Sure. Seven years ago."

He leaned against the counter. "It's different in the gay community."

Rue lifted an eyebrow.

"It is!" David insisted.

They were silent as Tug hopped onto the soggy couch. It was left over from the last tenants, a hideous yellow number from the 70's. Water squelched out of the cushions. Rue rubbed the throbbing space between her eyebrows.

"On a scale of one to ten, how mad are you?" David asked around bites.

She squinted at him. "I'd say a twelve."

"So now wouldn't be a good time to tell you my news?"

Rue reached out and took his yogurt, not bothering to get a new spoon. "This is terrible," she said, wincing at the taste of chalky cherries. "Good news or bad?"

A drop of condensation dripped off the ceiling and plopped on David's cheek. He swiped at it absently and shrugged. "Depends on who you are."

"Interesting. Let's assume I'm me."

He made a noncommittal sound and took back his terrible yogurt, suddenly too busy sloshing around underneath the sink for a trash bag to meet her eye.

Rue's heart sank. She knew what was coming. She'd had this conversation a hundred times, with her college boyfriend who'd fallen in love with his math tutor and her high school best friend who'd somehow gotten a full ride to Yale with a GPA of 3.4.

She was surprised her Luck had taken this long to rub off on David.

"Just tell me," she said.

"I got a gig!" he said, grinning at her, the trash bag forgotten in his hand.

She couldn't help but smile. David had been trying to break into acting for years. She'd lost count of the number of audition tapes he'd sent to agents over the years. Auditions for toothpaste commercials, HBO dramas, and weird indie films.

"Tell me all about it."

He did, in his David way. Waving his hands as he outlined the pilot for a gay sitcom he'd landed with FX. He told her about his co-star as he moved around the room tossing ruined things in the plastic bag. She was watching him empty the bottom shelf of the coffee table, which was filled with soggy self-help books she'd been meaning to read, when he got to the part about moving to LA.

He deflated, straightening. "I'm sorry, babe—but I promise I won't leave you high and dry."

Rue huffed at the joke despite the pit in her stomach. The problem with being Good Luck was that people were always running past her on their way to better things.

"It's okay," she lied. "The lease is up in the spring anyway and—"

Her phone rang.

Rue fumbled it out of her pocket. Her mom's face peered up at her from her lock screen. It was a picture she'd chosen after a rather vigorous round of lip filler, and it was so photoshopped that she was barely recognizable as a human, let alone a retired 61-year-old who played pickleball in Central Park on Wednesdays and loved her ancient Maltese way too much.

Rue considered not answering, but only for a second. Her mom was the most relentless person she knew. She made the "I need to take this call " face at David, and he nodded, splashing back to his bedroom without calling the landlord.

She sighed and picked up on the last ring.

"Happy Birthday, Ruth Ann!" her mom sang. "Am I bothering you? Are you getting ready for your big birthday bash?"

Rue had never had a birthday bash in her entire life. She was more of a one-friend-over-to-watch-a-movie-and-get-drunk kinda birthday girl. Or she would be if Bumble BFF had been even remotely successful—which it had not.

She secured the phone in the crook of her neck and decided lying was her best (and fastest) option to getting off the phone.

"Actually, Mom, I was just about to hop into the shower so..."

"Is that the nice boy you've been dating with you? I like him. The computer programmer? What's his name?"

Rue searched her memory for the last guy she'd told her mother about. "Ethan?"

"Yes!" her mom trilled.

"Mom, I'm not dating anyone right now."

This was an understatement. Ethan, the computer programmer, had invited her to lunch last Wednesday. A careful mid-week fourth date. The one that came right after the mediocre sex and before the comfortable relationship, but shockingly, he'd ghosted, leaving her sitting in a trendy cafe with an overpriced charcuterie board.

On the phone, Rue could hear a door open and then the familiar hollow sounds of the hot yoga studio her mom loved. "I'm sure you'll find someone who's even better tonight! You should wear that tight red dress..."

Wearily, Rue considered her flooded apartment. The water was already receding, soaking into the shitty carpet on its way to becoming black mold. Her only friend in the world was moving, and she was getting dumped by computer programmers.

Her chest tightened. She was twenty-seven, the age at which people were supposed to find the love of their life and settle into a meaningful career. The age where they met up with girlfriends on wine night to talk about wedding venues or complain about their boyfriends' video game addiction.

All she wanted to do tonight was watch old Pixar classics with an entire bag of Cool Ranch Doritos. To burrow back into her childhood for a night, where she'd never have to deal with flooded apartments or shitty boyfriends or the soul-crushing suspicion that no one would ever really love her.

Rue listened as her mom rambled on about the bitch in her book club and the corporate job opening she'd "heard about" from her friend Colleen.

"Fuck this," Rue whispered, sliding off the counter. The carpet squished underneath her socks. She peeled them off.

She might not have a gaggle of friends or even a sex buddy to hang out with on her birthday, but at least she could have a dry apartment. She'd seen the landlord earlier, so she knew he was around. Tug followed her to the door.

"... I know you said you don't want to try that Ozempic," her mom was saying, "but my Friday pickle ball friend—Sally?—she tried it. She said it was absolutely life-changing once she got past the nausea, and if you just lost a couple of pounds, I think it might help with—"

"Mom," Rue interrupted, grabbing Tug's leash.

Her mom didn't skip a beat. "Oh, Ruthie, I know everyone's all about that body positivity stuff, but if you would just do a little more to take care of yourself..."

Rue froze, one hand on the front doorknob, listening as her mom turned love into a weapon.

At 5'4" and slightly more ample than curvy, she'd never been considered pretty. She was the kind of girl trendy boudoir photographers could turn into a voluptuous bombshell with the right lighting. The type who needed things like sexy pictures to heal the insults that had sunk into her skin over the years.

Her jaw clenched. There was only so much a girl could take in one night.

"Rue, Mom," she said sharply. "I've gone by Rue for 15 years." She ignored the sputtering protest about her name and hung up before her mom could get in one more backhanded compliment. The tightness in her chest had become sharper, burning the back of her throat.

She looked down at Tug, whose snoot was fully touching the front door. His tail thwapped her side.

It was late. Past 9pm. And her slippers were filled with water.

"Let's go find Mikey," she told him. There were a hundred things wrong with her life, but at least she could fix a flooded apartment.

Two

Griff kept his cards face down against the flecked Formica table, ignoring the glares of the other men in the cramped kitchen.

He didn't bother to check his hand. He was holding two pair, which was good, but he'd gotten no help from the cards on the table. Despite the odds, he reached for his chips, tossing two more into the growing pile in the middle of the table.

Two thousand dollars. The highest bet of the night.

He flicked his eyes up to the other men without lifting his chin. "I raise."

Across from him, Mikey stubbed out his cigarette. It smoked in the overflowing ashtray, adding to the thick smoke circling their heads. Griff forced himself not to cough. He hadn't seen this much actual smoking in years, but this was a group of men who would never consider vaping or, god forbid, an edible.

To his left, a man with the battered fedora took a long drag from a stubby cigar as he considered his cards. His meaty fingers were stained with nicotine. A half dozen scratched gold rings choked the flesh below his knuckles.

The heavily bearded man to his right (names hadn't been asked or offered), muttered under his breath as he contemplated his hand. The words sounded a lot like "cheat" and "rat bastard." His thick eyebrows furrowed as he chewed on the inside of his cheek and glared.

Griff didn't bother reacting. The night was going precisely as planned, and he didn't expect them to be happy about it. Eventually, they each matched his bet the way too-proud men usually do.

He would have felt a little guilty beating the shit out of these men if he hadn't done a deep dive into their sleazy business dealings, which included a little gunrunning and a lot of shadowy real estate dealings. The way things layed, he was practically Robin Hood.

Griff watched silently as Mikey (the clear boss and "brains" of the operation) flipped over the river card. The man's eyebrow twitched at the revealed ace, a subtle tell, but the bearded man swore and folded violently, scattering his cards across the table.

Fedora was slower to decide, studying Griff with shrewd eyes. He was younger than the other two, in his late fifties ,and muscular beneath his straining shirt . His fedora might have been a prop from a Spirit Halloween if the rim hadn't been dented and sweat-stained from years of use. It was the kind of hat that had seen things. Probably murder.

Griff kept his face relaxed as the dangerous men decided if he was bluffing. The seconds stretched. The only sound was the occasional blare of a taxi horn from the cracked apartment window and the too-heavy breath of men that should have stopped smoking twenty years ago.

Tonight's game hadn't started so quietly. The three men had piled into the apartment like old friends, all loud, boastful lies about women they were too old to fuck amongst hearty back slaps. The food had been pierogis—potato and cabbage—greasy and served hot from styrofoam containers on the kitchen counter. The booze, though, had been top shelf.

This wasn't Mikey's home, of course. The Rolex watches and Italian leather shoes were enough of a clue to know that these mafia wannabes had a penthouse in a better neighborhood, not to mention a second home where the taxes were sheltered, and the sun was warm.

This was just an empty apartment in one of Mikey's many run-down tax shelters. The poker table was the only furniture in the place, and there wasn't so much as a bar of soap in the bathroom. The kitchen trash was filled with empty bottles of Jim Beam, and the place stank of body odor and expensive cologne.

Griff glanced at the heavy diamond ring on Mikey's thick finger. Apparently, being a slumlord was good money.

"You'd fold if you knew what was good for you," Mikey said gruffly, tapping one finger on the table, as if he was just giving friendly advice.

Griff knew a fake "tell" when he saw one. He ignored the finger tap, keeping his tone mild. "Is that so?"

Mikey had beady black eyes over a heavy brow. There was nothing but a lifetime of cruelty and privilege in those eyes, unless you counted the bleariness of too much alcohol. Still, rage flickered past the man's poker face for long enough that Griff was grateful for the small pistol tucked in his waistband.

They hadn't bothered to search him when he'd arrived, but that had been confidence rather than trust. If he pulled anything, there was no chance he would leave this dark, musty apartment alive.

He was going to win tonight, but he had to do it carefully. These were not the kind of men who took losing kindly.

After several more minutes of grumbling, Fedora folded too, calling Griff several unpleasant names around his last sip of scotch. Mikey just leaned back in his chair. It creaked in protest.

"You seem confident," Griff observed mildly, picking up his hand and studying it as if he didn't have it memorized.

It was the first unprovoked information he'd offered all night. Mikey's eyebrow twitched again. It was one of Griff's favorite late-game strategies. People hated being perceived, especially poker players. It was a surprisingly effective way to unsettle an opponent.

"You're a smug bastard, aren't ya?" Mikey answered, folding his hands calmly on top of his cards. He shrugged. "I'm not scared of a little punk."

"No?"

Mikey leered, one gold tooth flashing. "I've got me a lucky charm."

Ah. Griff relaxed. If there was one thing he knew after years of playing cards, it was that superstitious men were stupid and almost all poker players were superstitious.

"You got some sort of rabbit's foot you bought in Tibet or some shit?" he asked.

On his right, Beard's bloodshot eyes narrowed. He was easily the drunkest of the lot. "No, you little shit. Mike's got a bona fide good luck charm. She's—"

Mikey's fist slammed on the table, making the poker chips jump and scatter. Scotch splashed on the green felt.

"Sal, when will you learn to shut your fucking mouth?" Mikey growled, showing real emotion for the first time since the perogies were eaten.

Beard held out his palms, eyes wide. "What? I didn't say nothin."

Griff just raised an eyebrow at Mikey. "She?"

Mikey took a swig, and then wiped his lips with the back of his hand. "Just this girl I've been fucking. She's my little lucky charm—not much to look at—a little chunky for my taste, but what the hell."

Griff gritted his teeth. Mikey was pushing seventy. His face was covered in liver spots, and his belly hung over his expensive belt. Griff guessed the man hadn't successfully used his dick in a decade.

Now he *knew* he was going to win. Mikey and his shady cronies were more gullible than Griff's usual opponents—half-drunk and sloppy with their money in the way only the outrageously rich could be. Superstition was just the nail in the coffin.

Mikey glared at him. Griff leaned back, crossing his ankles and smiled.

He was wearing all black, from the tip of his scuffed boots to the collar of the overpriced vintage t-shirt. He had unremarkable gray eyes and brown hair that curled against his neck when it got too long, but he had a decent face. Lean, with a straight nose and good jaw line, he looked best with a bit of scruff. His

Griff knew the old man saw the smug smirk of the twenty-five-year-old he had been back in his glory days. Saw the face that made beautiful girls look twice, and the body that knew how to fuck them.

Mikey took another puff on his cigar, taking it slow to prove he was the one in control, and then pushed the rest of his chips into the middle of the table. Griff's heart stuttered. He had to work to keep his face neutral.

The pot was over 50k. The river card had completed his full house, a hand that was nearly impossible to beat.

Griff considered the distance from the poker table to the front door and then flipped his cards. The tips of his fingers tingled, effervescence bubbling in his chest. There was nothing like winning. It was even better when it really mattered. When—

Across the table, Mikey chuckled. Griff blinked. The rush of adrenaline coursing through his veins turned to ice.

No.

It wasn't possible.

Mikey tossed his hand onto the stack of chips. Griff stared at it in bewilderment. The bastard had a straight flush—a statistical anomaly.

Fedora whooped and shoved Mikey in the shoulder, tipping his chair onto the floor with a bang. Beard boomed with laughter.

Stunned, Griff leaned back, running his hand through his hair. He'd lost. Either he had miscounted or they had cheated, which was harder than it sounded and unlikely considering their arrogance.

Fedora wiggled his fingers in the universal "pay up" gesture. Griff reached for the stack of cash in his inside pocket, ignoring the insults from the two goons as he counted out money he couldn't afford to lose.

Mikey's beady eyes glittered. He grinned and it was all teeth. "Don't feel bad, kid. You had balls to come here tonight."

Wordless, Griff stood, retrieving his jacket from the back of the chair.

"Who are you, son?" Mikey asked as Fedora silently counted the money.

The son part was an insult, but Griff didn't bite. If there was one thing he knew about these kind of men, it was that one type of winning would never be enough. They wouldn't be happy until he was bloody in an alley. Or dead.

He wasn't getting out of here without answering a few questions, so he gave the same answer he always gave. The one that was both a truth and a lie.

"I'm just a guy."

"The fuck you are," Beard snarled, swaying slightly.

"I play online. This is, um, my first...you know," Griff stumbled over the words on purpose, trying to slip smoothly from confident poker player to shucks-golly kid as quickly as possible. "It's my first in-person game."

Mikey looked up from the chips. "Bullshit."

It was. Griff tried to look dejected and small as he inched toward the door. "Guess I'll just stick to online games."

The henchmen followed, but Mikey didn't bother standing up or turning around.

"Don't come back here," he said quietly.

It was not a threat. It was business. Griff's death would be a transaction as sound as a contract signed.

He nodded at the back of the man's head. "You'll never see me again."

It was a promise he wasn't planning on keeping.

Three

The man on the stairs was holding a stack of hundred-dollar bills.

He looked up when she appeared on the steps below him, but didn't bother hiding the money he'd been counting. Rue hesitated. She was barefoot and unarmed, but she was also with Tug, and even though *she* knew her dog wouldn't hurt a kitten (Tug loved kittens), his size gave her a certain amount of bravery.

The man held up both hands in surrender when he saw Tug, the stack of money still gripped in his fist, but he didn't look particularly dangerous. Even under the fluorescent lights, he was attractive, with nondescript gray eyes and an overgrown mop of wavy brown hair that contrasted with his neatly trimmed beard.

He wore the same black jeans and AC/DC t-shirt every man their age bought from Target, but there was something about the outfit that screamed: I have money. Maybe it was the Rolex, dangling from his wrist like an afterthought, or the straight white teeth.

Mentally, Rue swiped right, despite herself. Out loud, her face frowned. "Who are you?"

The man didn't seem bothered by being questioned by a soggy stranger in a half-abandoned apartment complex. He gave her a half smile that was annoyingly adorable. "Door dash?"

She nodded at the stack of cash. "I didn't realize my landlord was such a good tipper."

The man glanced down, as if surprised that he was still holding thousands of dollars. A few strands of hair slipped in front of his eyes, and he gave a little head shake before slipping the wad of cash into his jacket pocket.

"Are you with the HOA? Community watch?" he teased. "Because I'm harmless."

"That's what all murderers say."

He laughed. "I'm not a murder-y kind of guy."

The man looked good when he laughed. Crinkles appeared beside his eyes, even though he looked a few years shy of thirty, and his aura loosened in a way that made her think he would be very good at sex. Playful and talented at the same time—the perfect combo.

Rue was suddenly painfully aware that she looked like a wet rat (if said rat also had frizzy hair and a birthday zit on her chin). The floodwater had soaked her jeans almost to her hip, and she was covered in dog hair. The name tag from her work was still pinned to her chest.

Dear god.

"Is Mr. Moratti up there?" she snapped, gesturing at the floor above him. She was never going to find out how good this guy was in bed anyway.

"You mean Mikey?"

She nodded, wrapping Tug's leash around her fingers a second time to keep him close.

Something odd flashed across the stranger's face. He glanced upward, his brow furrowing for the first time. "Are you...are you his girlfriend?"

Rue blinked once and then burst out laughing. Mr. Moratti was old enough to be her father, not to mention an alcoholic with sagging jowls. The fact that this cute stranger thought she was fucking her landlord was the cherry on top of an already terrible day.

"He's my landlord," she said. "I'm having some, um, apartment issues."

"Ah. That explains the...dampness."

Rue refused to look down at herself. She was well aware of how pathetic she currently looked.

"Well, I'll let you get to it," cute-guy-she-was-never-going-to-sleep-with said, moving aside on the small landing.

She tried to squeeze past him quickly, but Tug stopped to smell the tip of his boots, forcing her to pause. The man smelled like cigarettes. It wasn't a nice smell, she told herself, watching as he patted Tug's head and noticing the easy way he held his body—as if the world belonged to him. It probably did.

"Hey, you might want to find a bank," she said. "They have them on every corner. Cool place to keep your money."

He laughed quietly, and it was charming as fuck.

"Any chance I could get your number?" he asked, glancing up from scratching Tug's chin.

Surprised, she blushed, but she was already shaking her head internally. She smelled like mildew. Her hair had turned into a Brillo pad, and there was a cat scratch on her cheek.

Dear lord, men would screw anything that breathed.

"I don't think that's a good idea," she replied, pulling Tug's leash.

Men were historically terrible at rejection, but this one just studied her for another moment, hands in his pockets, as if giving her a chance to change her mind.

There was something about his soft gray eyes that almost succeeded, but then he just nodded slowly and said, "Fair enough."

"Have a nice night," she said, turned away from those earnest, searching eyes.

***

Griff waited in the shadows until the girl with the green eyes and horse dog went back down to their flooded apartment. He waited until Mikey and Fedora stumbled down the stairs to the black sedan, the smell of body odor and cigar smoke lingering even after their brake lights glowed red. He waited until the cold night turned frigid.

He flicked up his coat collar, trying not to shiver. A stakeout hadn't been part of tonight's plan. He should be driving home with a quarter million dollars in a suspicious-looking briefcase, the windows cracked to let in the crisp January air. He'd even picked out a victory playlist for the drive.

Instead, he was standing in the cold at 2am, in a shitty neighborhood.

Beard was the last to leave Mikey's apartment, swaying on the welcome mat while he fumbled with the keys. A white trash bag clinked in his left hand. His suit jacket was a crumpled ball underneath his sweat-stained armpit, exposing the gun holster at his side.

Griff supposed even gangsters had to take out the garbage.

He pressed deep into the shadows as the man passed and then followed silently, but there was no need really. Beard held his phone awkwardly clamped between his ear and shoulder, nodding and garbling "yes, sir" as he lumbered down the stairs. Griff could have been wearing tap shoes, and the man probably wouldn't have noticed.

At the ground floor, Beard turned through the breezeway, past the pretty girl's flooded apartment, and headed for the parking lot in the back of the complex. Griff waited as the man tossed the trash into the dumpster and then paused underneath the street light, still talking on the phone. It wasn't until Beard finished the conversation that Griff stepped from the shadows.

It only takes a split second to steal a drunk man's gun. Beard had barely gotten out a surprised garble before the muzzle was pressed against the fatty flab underneath his chin. To his credit, the man didn't flinch.

"Damn it," Beard slurred, squinting even though they stood a foot apart.

"Yeah. Damn it," Griff responded, taking the phone from the man's hand and slipping it into his own pocket.

"My boss will kill you for this," Beard sneered. One meaty fist curled at his side, but he wasn't stupid enough to try to use it.

Griff snorted. "I doubt he'd waste resources on someone like you."

Beard's eyes flared. The insult hit a little too close to home.

"Fuck you," he spat. His breath was sour.

Griff nuzzled the gun deeper into Beard's soft neck. "Besides, you're not going to tell him."

Beard grinned, and it was all teeth. "Why would I keep quiet?"

"Because you're going to tell me about Mikey's lucky charm."

Beard stopped smiling. "Why would I do that?"

Griff wiggled the gun. "I think it's pretty obvious."

Beard eyed him shrewdly, his gaze no longer blurry. It was amazing what real danger could do to a drunk, and Griff wasn't foolish enough to think that danger was the gun in his hand.

"He'd kill me," Beard said.

Griff flicked off the safety. "I won't tell."

Beard sneered and glared and spat on the cold concrete, but finally said, "The lucky bitch lives in the basement apartment of this shit hole. Mikey runs a background check on every tenant, just in case. He found out some...history of note about young Miss Adler."

Griff's mind flashed back to the soggy girl from the stairs. She had pretty eyes, but otherwise looked like every other twenty-something in line at Starbucks. Well, except for the wet clothes and comically large dog.

"And?" Griff coaxed, wanting more.

Beard shrugged. "There are stories. News articles and shit. A few years back, she was holed up in this podunk town in the Midwest, and folks found out she could cure cancer or win them the lotto. People started hanging out in her yard. Bothering her at work. And then one day she just...disappeared."

"So Mikey thinks this girl is some sort of talisman? Like a damn four-leaf clover?" Griff scoffed.

"If you don't believe me, then why are you here?"

A car pulled into the apartment parking lot. Griff tucked the gun back into his waistband as the headlights swept over them. Neither of them moved as a tired woman in blue scrubs got out of her car, giving them a cursory glance before disappearing into the apartment complex.

"I shouldn't have lost that game," Griff said.

Beard's gaze narrowed. "You counting cards, boy?"

Griff tossed Beard back his phone. "I guess we're all cheaters here."

Four

"Home is where somebody notices when you are no longer there."—Aleksander Hamon

"You sure you're going to be okay?" David asked. He was standing in the living room with his suitcases, looking worried as men in respirator masks and stained ball caps that said "Don's Carpet Cleaning" dodged around them.

The cleaners had been there all day, ripping up wet carpet and setting up industrial fans. Their hazmat suits annoyed Rue more than having to evacuate her apartment for a few days. Sure, her apartment smelled like day-old washing machine clothes, but it wasn't like they were here to clean up a dead body for fuck sake.

"I'll be fine!" she lied, plastering on a smile. "You go show LA who's boss!"

He looked doubtful but let her shoo him out the door. Tug dancing between them on the sidewalk as the Uber pulled up behind the carpet truck.

David was already dressed for Hollywood, with a fresh haircut and salmon colored polo. He shivered, but had refused to take his coat to the airport. In a couple hours, he'd be in California. She was donating all his winter clothes.

They'd never been much more than good roommates, but seeing him standing there with his suitcase still made her chest ache. She knew what would happen next. She'd been left behind a dozen times before. People moved past her, using her luck as a stepping stone to launch themselves into something better.

It wasn't malicious. David would text her, for fun at first, then out of guilt—daily, and then less and less. She'd like his Instagrams, and he'd reply with a kissing emoji until he decided to go on a social media cleanse three years from now, and then they would lose track of each other, and that would be that.

Soon, he'd be someone she used to know.

"Do you want to share an Uber?" David asked while the Uber driver tossed his luggage into the trunk of a Honda Accord. "I could drop you at your hotel."

Rue dodged to the side as a man carrying a long silver hose squeezed past her on the sidewalk. "Nah, I think I'll walk. It's a nice day, and Tug needs it."

She watched, numb, as David said goodbye to his dog. They'd never discussed out loud who would keep Tug. He'd been a puppy when David moved in three years ago, all long legs and ears and bounding enthusiasm. She'd fallen in love instantly.

Rue suspected David considered Tug a consolation prize for abandoning her, even though he was moving into a condo with four other actors and wasn't remotely equipped to take care of anything living. Especially a 120-pound Great Dane.

Regardless, she was glad someone in her life couldn't leave.

The rest of the goodbye was painfully quick. Soon, David's Uber had turned the corner, and it was just her and the sound of the industrial fan. Tug leaned against her hip, his head wedged underneath her arm.

It felt heavier than usual, resting there.

"It's okay, buddy," she said, rubbing his velvet ear. "We've got each other."

***

The shelter's back door was unlocked even though it was after hours. Rue slipped inside quietly, glancing up at the security camera in the corner and giving it a little wave while Tug tippy-tapped happily beside her. The hall lights flickered twice—a hello from whichever kennel tech was working the evening shift.

Her office was closest to the back door, and the little brass plaque beside it had her name on it:

Ruth Ann Adler
Adoptions Manager

It was still weird to see it there, even though she'd been promoted almost a year ago. Ruth Ann Adler sounded like a different person. Like someone with a career and a wine fridge and an IRA. Someone with her life together.

It was a stressful job. Their little non-profit shelter always seemed on the verge of closing, and after the generosity of the holidays passed, things got worse. In January, it was hard to keep the free dog pantry filled with donations, and there was a constant stream of animals that needed a safe place to stay.

She loved every minute. Loved standing beside hopeful dogs at community adoption events and bottle feeding kittens late into the night. It was rewarding, exhausting, and sometimes heartbreaking work.

Rue shouldered open the office door, her hands overloaded with the (slightly damp) blanket she'd brought from home, her duffle bag, and two overflowing Trader Joe's bags. Tug barged into the room next to her, nearly knocking her sideways on his way to do a careful sniffspection of the office.

She'd considered getting a hotel while they fixed the apartment, but her bank account had protested the cost of a pet-friendly hotel for even for a couple nights. Her office was windowless, like most of the shelter, which had been built as a World War II bunker. She'd tried to brighten the grim space with a floor lamp and cheerful yellow rug, but it had been only partially successful. The snake plant in the corner was dying despite the grow lamp, and there was a musty smell she couldn't seem to get rid of, no matter how many candles she lit.

Tug didn't seem to notice, helping himself to a soggy lamb chop toy a shelter dog had left behind. He jumped onto the couch, spun twice, and settled into one corner.

"Don't get comfortable," Rue warned, dumping her stuff on her messy desk. "I have to sleep there."

She was not looking forward to it. The couch was lumpy and smelled like dog. Tug ignored her, happily gnawing on the toy.

"Stay off the desk," she sighed before leaving.

She closed the door behind her and headed deeper into the shelter. Her footsteps echoed on the spotless concrete floors, and soft music played through the speakers, something light and jazzy that would soothe the animals. The fluorescent lights chased away any shadows. Still, there was a perpetual heaviness in the air, despite the cheerful posters of children adopting puppies and the big window that looked in on the "featured" cats.

Nothing could quite erase the despair of a place where creatures were forgotten.

There were more obvious signs, too, hidden away from potential adoptees. A basket of used leashes that were too nice to throw away, and the stack of cardboard boxes from the countless nameless parking lot drop-offs. Rue suppressed a shiver as she passed the sterile room where the sickest dogs went but never left.

There were some parts of this job that everyone hated.

She walked through the dark lobby, grabbing a handful of treats from the jar on the front desk before pushing open the heavy door that separated the dog room from the rest of the shelter. It was quieter than usual, even at full occupancy. There were a few barks—big, scary, gruff ones mixed with a staccato of tiny yaps, but most of the dogs were asleep—exhausted by a life they hadn't chosen and didn't deserve.

Rue checked the clipboard that hung on a hook next to the door. There were 47 guests, which meant there had been 8 intakes over the weekend and only 3 adoptions.

She frowned. The staff had been inundated with dozens of inevitable adoption fails when families discovered that keeping an animal was more than just making cute Christmas videos to post online. Their shelter had the third-highest adoption rate in the whole country, thanks to a little extra Luck, but nothing was perfect.

Rue wandered down the first row of cages, pausing to visit each occupant, kneeling to touch soft foreheads and allow enthusiastic licks on whatever part of her they could wiggle through the bars.

It got louder as the dogs realized she was offering treats and love. The noise drilled into the headache she'd been nursing, but she kept her shoulders easy and her smile soft. Dogs could sense tension, and these creatures didn't need any of her pain.

She was playing a gentle game of tug-of-war with a ratty old shih tzu named Muppet when the door to the dog room snicked open behind her.

A few seconds later, Addie, the night shift attendant, appeared wearing a rainbow Snuggie. She was a pretty college student with aspirations to become a vet, a bad case of cystic acne, and shockingly blue eyes. She was holding a clipboard.

"Check on Cage 37," she said around a yawn. "Came in late Friday night. Postpartum mom with no pups. We're calling her Hecate."

Rue's knees cracked as she stood. The German Shepherd mix in the next cage sniffed her shoes, waiting patiently for his treat. "As in the Goddess Hecate?"

Addie grinned. "Yup."

"Good name," Rue said, slipping a treat through the bars to the too-thin Shepherd.

"It's the least we can do for them," Addie replied softly. Anger flashed over her face, strangely out of place. She was the kind of girl who normally made jokes to soothe the pain and dressed the dogs in cute costumes for social media, but eventually the despair got to them all.

"Turnip?" Rue asked.

"He's had a few meet and greets over the weekend, but no takers."

Turnip, a long-term resident who was more potato than dog, had been in the shelter for 178 days. Round and white, with fur somewhere between straggly and bare, he had the personality of Napoleon Bonaparte—but only if the former general farted a lot. The bulldog mix was a cancer survivor, the scar on his round belly puckered and red. Over time, it had faded, but he had stayed despite her best attempts to find him a home. Sometimes, even Luck wasn't enough.

As Addie started her rounds in the cat room, Rue continued down the second row of dogs, paying extra attention to the quiet ones and tossing toys to the bouncing pups.

She'd seen the question in Addie's eyes, but everyone had been instructed not to ask her any questions. Sandra, the shelter's owner, was the only one who officially knew about Rue's special talent, and even she'd been skeptical until the adoption numbers started to rise. Last fall, Good Morning America had done a fluff piece on the King County Shelter's astonishing success story.

It would be time to move on soon. She couldn't risk getting noticed. The thought made her stomach hurt.

Rue lowered herself in front of cage 37. The concrete was cold under her knees.

A Golden peered at her from a tight knot in the corner, half hidden underneath a knot of fleece blankets. Her hair tangled and matted from neglect, her belly still round from her absent babies. Rue could smell her, a combination of piss and filth.

"Hey, beautiful Mama," Rue whispered, unlatching the cage. Hecate's tail began to slowly wag, but her soft brown eyes remained weary and distrustful.

It took Rue forty minutes to coax the sweet girl from the corner and another twenty before the mama crawled into her arms. By 10 pm, they were snuggling, Ruth's back pressed against the cage walls, her arms filled with stinky dog. Hecate was heavy despite the frail ladder of her ribs.

"100%"

Startled, Rue looked up at the girl standing outside the cage. She'd pulled the hood up on her Snuggie and was clutching a bag of dog food with both arms.

"What?" Rue asked.

"That's how many of the dogs you visit get adopted," Addie said quietly.

Rue knew this, of course. It was why she sat with them. It's also why she was welcome at the children's cancer ward downtown, and the hospice center on Oakwood Street, and the county prison.

"Weird," Rue replied, shifting, as the Golden sighed in her arms.

Addie smiled softly. "Yeah. Weird."

Five

"I'm leaving."

Rue started awake, lifted her head off the front desk, and squinted at Addie as morning light streamed through the foyer windows. The girl looked like a witch without her rainbow Snuggie—if a witch had been assembled from pieces of a cottage core Instagram account and was also a tiny mouse.

Rue scrubbed a hand across her face and yawned. A paperclip peeled off her cheek and plinked back onto the desk.

She'd been sleeping at the shelter for three nights, due to what Mr. Moretti called—unforeseen circumstances with the construction. After the first night, she couldn't stomach the lumpy couch, so she'd been sleeping in the cushy desk chair in the lobby. It wasn't much better.

"What time is it?" Rue asked, casting around the desk for her water bottle.

"7 am," Addie replied. Her blond hair was brushed out and soft. Her lips shone with gloss. "I'm heading out early, remember? I've got the weekend off."

Rue realized that she was wearing the same coffee-stained sweats from the first night. "You got a boyfriend or something?"

As if on cue, someone rapped lightly on the front door. Rue turned as the American version of Timothy Chalamet stepped inside the shelter, holding a bouquet of wildflowers so large she could barely see more than the top of his curly head.

Addie squeaked, spinning and leaping into the boy's arms like a girl in a damn rom-com. Flowers went everywhere, an explosion of daisies and pink peonies scattered across the lobby floor as the boy swung the girl around, nearly knocking down the rack of spay/neuter brochures.

Rue stood awkwardly, desperately aware of the rancid taste inside her mouth and the carpet of dog hair coating her sweatshirt.

The lovers were oblivious. When the kissing was done, Addie turned back to her, bright as the morning sun, holding what was left of the bouquet with one hand and the boy's hand with the other.

"Is it okay if I...If we..." she asked breathlessly.

Rue waved a hand as if there weren't flower petals blowing around the foyer and a shelter full of dogs who needed breakfast. "Of course!"

Her voice came out a little wistful, but they didn't seem to notice, rushing out the door in a nauseating flurry of giggles. Rue

watched the boy give Addie another passionate kiss on the sidewalk
before tucking her into his beat-up Subaru.

Silence descended on the shelter immediately, as if Addie had
taken all sparkle and light left in the world with her. Even the quiet
music playing overhead sounded like a dirge. Ruth clicked it off.

She tried not to think as she cleaned up in the lobby bathroom
and then moved through the kennel, petting heads and doling out
kibble. It was hard work, and after an hour, she headed across the
lobby to the medical area. A chorus of gruff barks greeted her, but
the room was quieter than the others. These were the sickest and
most tender animals.

Rue did her rounds, pausing in front of her favorite tomcat.
The orange old lady was curled in the back of the crate, her nose
squished tightly into the corner. Charlotte hadn't touched her
food, even though Rue added some real canned tuna to the top of
her kibble.

"Hey sweetie," she whispered, flicking open the cage. Charlotte
meowed softly, her voice soft and broken. She'd been surrendered
a few days ago at the age of fourteen when the only mom she'd
ever known had been admitted to a nursing home. The sweet old
lady had made them promise to take good care of her baby. It was
a promise Rue intended to keep.

"Are you sad this morning?" Rue asked, holding out her hand.
Charlotte gave it a sidelong glance before pressing her face back
into the corner.

She closed the crate gently, respecting the old girl's space. She
wondered what it would be like to be Lucky for so long, only to

lose it at the very end. That must be worse than never being lucky at all, right?

Turnip was in the last cage. He was their longest resident. He'd also been their sickest. Not that you could tell by the way he was sprawled upside down on the concrete. His tongue flopped over his wrinkled cheek, nearly touching the floor as he snored.

"Hey, ya baked potato," Rue said. His stubby tail started wagging when she unlatched his cage, but he didn't flip over. She rolled her eyes and hefted him into her arms. He only weighed 50 pounds, but it felt like 100. He did not help, limp in her arms, as she took him out to the lobby.

After the Uber Eats driver dropped off her Starbucks, she sat at the desk with her feet up, playing on her phone while Turnip slobber-breathed against her neck. The shelter didn't open for another hour and—

The bell above the shelter's front door jingled as it swung open. "Ruthie! My sweet baby!"

Rue blinked, standing slowly, as her mom shook snow from her perfectly coiffed gray hair.

"Mom?"

Her mom's arms were filled with belated Christmas presents. "Where can I put these down?"

Before Rue could answer, her mom clicked across the lobby on her completely impractical high heels as if this were the Upper East Side and not Portland, Oregon. The pile of gifts tumbled onto the front desk. One bag tipped over, revealing a shoe box with a conspicuous Gucci label on the side. Her mom didn't notice or care, patting her hair one more time before rushing in for a hug.

Her fur coat tickled Rue's nose, but she couldn't help but sink into the embrace, squeezing her eyes closed and breathing in the smell of roses and the menthol cigarettes her mom swore she'd given up years ago.

Turnip snuffed unhappily between them.

"Mom," she said, her voice muffled by the fur. "Why are you not in New York?"

Her mom pulled back. Her mouth frowned, but her forehead stayed firmly in place. "Are you not happy to see me?"

Rue's chest tightened. "Mom, I'm...I'm always happy to see you. Of course! But you didn't mention—"

Her mom waved a hand. "Ruth Ann Adler, I don't have to run everything by you anymore. We're both adults. Can't I come see my..."

She paused, peering into Rue's face as if trying to read a map upside-down. "Dear, you look terrible."

"That's...Mom, you can't say that to people."

Her mom swiped at Rue's hair, trying to rearrange it into something she would find acceptable. "I'm not people, Ruthie. I'm your mother!"

Rue flashed the smile she always used with her mom. The one that felt like paper. "Just wondering why you are six hundred miles from home."

Her mom waved that hand again, the enormous engagement ring she'd been wearing the last six years catching on the Christmas lights as she idly patted Turnip's head. "Tim and I are on our way to Maui for the winter. Feliz Navidad or whatever they say there. I thought I'd stop and hug my daughter."

Something inside Rue shifted and tumbled at that casual statement. Her mom had never visited her—not once in the past three years. Rue was suddenly very tired. Grief tickled the back of her throat. Her mom didn't notice, prattling on about Tim's failing stocks and the bitchy girl at the gym.

"Mom," Rue interrupted. "Do you have them?"

Her mom pressed her lips together, one manicured hand resting on the desk. Her eyes were shrewd in a way that was as familiar as the smell of menthol. Ruth expected her to protest, but she had the decency not to pretend as she pulled a stack of lottery tickets from her designer pocketbook.

She smiled, and it was sticky. "Do you mind, dearest?"

She did. Rue minded down to the marrow of her bones, but she stood silently as her mom arranged the tickets on the front desk, patting her arm before scratching each one with the Lucky silver dollar she kept in her wallet as if Rue wasn't enough, even for this.

Neither one of them bothered to check the results. They'd win. Not the millions that got too much attention and ruined lives, but just enough to keep Mom and Tim in their Upper East Side apartment. The one with the nice doorman, rooftop pool, and sterile lobby.

Her mom patted Rue's cheek. "Such a good girl you are, Ruth Ann, my little good luck charm."

Rue forced herself to smile. There were many things a good daughter could be for a mother, but useful was not the one that mattered.

They pretended for a little longer, dancing through belated Christmas gifts and dry kisses before her mom disappeared back into the snow with a cheerful wave. Rue locked the shelter door behind her, watching as her mom got into the Lexus waiting at the curb. Tim pulled away, waving out the driver's window as they left the parking lot.

Rue didn't move for a long time, watching the snow cover up the tire tracks until it was if no one had been there at all.

***

It was early Monday morning, but there was already a line at the shelter. The girl at the desk was wearing a rainbow Snuggie and holding a potato-shaped dog under one arm.

Griff waited impatiently while she helped an old lady fill out paperwork for the senior cat meowing relentlessly in the crate at her feet, although he could barely hear it over the cacophony of barks coming from a heavy door marked "Dog Room."

Other than the noise, the Rue Adler's shelter looked clean and well-loved. A little kid in a Batman hoodie was standing on his tiptoes to see inside a big window where a collection of orange kittens were frolicking. Bright posters decorated the concrete walls, announcing past adoption events, and a collage of polaroids featuring a Noah's ark of animals, each posing with its new parents, was pinned to the wall behind the desk.

Griff browsed an article taped to the front of the desk as the old lady grilled the desk girl about her new cat's gluten-free diet. He noticed Rue's name immediately and leaned closer to read. Apparently, Muddy Paws had the third-highest adoption rate in the country, just behind a shelter in central LA and a TikTok-famous one in New York.

The journalist mused on the reason, wondering why the pets were so lucky in this small, independent shelter. Griff was starting to have an idea.

He hadn't planned on researching Rue Adler after his little "meeting" with Beard. He didn't believe in good luck charms. Superstition was just a mind trick to help a person overcome their own fear and self-doubt.

Still, here he was, trying to get some dirt on Ms. Lucky Charm.

"Sorry about that! Can I help you?" the desk girl said brightly. The crooked name tag pinned to her snuggie said "Abbie."

Griff gave her his most winning smile. "I was hoping to look at the dogs?"

He wasn't. The last thing he needed right now was another thing to keep alive, but it was an easy lie. He wasn't planning on leaving here with anything but info.

"Any breed? Energy level?" The potato dog underneath Addie's arm started squirming, so she set it down on the cluttered desk. It appeared to be some sort of bulldog, if said bulldog was the result of a terrible genetic accident.

"A Lab?" he said, looking down at the potato. It had a face like Napoleon and a pink scar on its belly. It sniffed his hand and then sneezed. Snot flew everywhere. Griff grimaced and wiped his hand on his jeans.

Labrador was the opposite of whatever this was. It was the most dog, dog he could think of.

Addie reached for a carabiner filled with keys before leaning over and hefting an enormous bag of kibble into her arms. It was nearly the same size as her torso. She peered at him over the top of the bag. "We've got some good mixes right now. A cute boy named Rocko, who's been here for a few weeks. He's mostly Pit, but he has some black lab in him, too. He's a snuggly guy, though—not much of an outdoorsman, if that's what you're looking for."

He was looking for nothing. Griff waved what he hoped was an indecisive hand. "Whatever, I'm just browsing."

"Cool. If you'll follow me, I'll take you..." She fumbled with the keys, bobbling the bag, and then smiled apologetically. "Actually, can you grab Turnip for me? I've got my hands full here."

Griff had a sinking feeling that the sneezing potato was Turnip. He opened his mouth to protest, but she'd already turned away, waving at the boy with the Batman hoodie as she jingled over to the dog room.

Turnip stared up at him. Drool dripped from his protruding tongue onto a pile of mail. Griff forced himself not to wrinkle his nose. He was supposed to be a dog guy. Or at least that was the con.

The potato snuffed when Griff picked him up, snuggling into his chest. Its labored breath was hot and sloppy but not entirely unpleasant. His fur was surprisingly soft, and there was something stupidly adorable about all the wrinkles.

"Don't get any ideas," Griff warned the dog.

Turnip fart happily. It smelled like chili.

"Jesus, you stink," Griff hissed as he followed Addie inside the dog room. Turnip licked his ear.

"Okay," she gasped, hefting the bag of dog food onto a growing donation pile. "Let me show you Rocko."

She kept talking as she led him deeper into the room, gesturing at various dogs that might fit his interest. It was a litany of heartbreak stories that became harder to hear after the first couple. He followed her down the line of cages, his steps getting slower with each dog he passed.

There were so many choices. Big shaggy dogs with unkempt fur and little shivering ones with ripped ears. Piles of tumbling puppies and old dogs with sugar faces and watchful, wary eyes. There was a too-thin Dalmatian straight out of a children's firetruck book and a mutt so mixed it had an overbite that looked like a grin.

Eventually, Griff stopped in front of one of the cages. It held a small crescent-shaped fluff, pressed into the darkest corner. The dog stared at him from the shadows, brown and young with a white spot across half its shaggy face. There was a medical sign zip-tied to the metal bars: quarantine. His name was Murphy, and he had heartworms.

Murphy's tail gave one wag when Addie came back to stand next to Griff, but the dog didn't bother getting up, as if he knew a pet wasn't in his near future.

"How do you do this?" he said. It wasn't what he meant to say. He meant to casually mention Rue, get some dirt on her and go, but the question just slipped out. In his arms, Turnip was snoring, a loud gasp-y slobbery sound as if he was breathing underwater.

"First time in a shelter?" Addie asked gently.

Griff shrugged.

He expected her to say something rehearsed and sympathetic, but instead she said, "These dogs have been used and cast aside, sir. It's our job to give them a place to rest until someone can promise them something better. We take that very seriously ."

Turnip shifted in his sleep, his soft ear brushing Griff's cheek. He needed to get out of here.

"Does...Rue Adler work here?" he asked, interrupting. the churning in his chest.

Addie blinked, her friendly expression shuttering immediately. "You know Rue?"

He flashed her his best charming aw-shucks smile. "I was chatting with her on Hinge. She convinced me to adopt a dog."

Addie studied him for a moment and then reached out to gather Turnip. The dog rolled over like a fat log in her arms, stretching his stubby legs. She scratched his pink belly and kissed his piggy nose. "Let's go see Rocko."

Suddenly, Griff didn't want to see Rocko, but he followed her down the line of cages anyway, nodding politely as she showed him the cute lab mix at the end of the row and trying to remember the real reason he'd come to Rue's shelter.

Six

Griff held out for another 24 hours before he found himself lurking on Luck's doorstep. He didn't believe in magic—not the kind that granted miracles. Good fortune came from hard work and skill.

Still, here he was, standing outside of some random girl's apartment, like a desperate man clutching a Powerball ticket. Some things were too important to be left to chance.

Griff was leaning against his BMW, hands deep in the pockets of his coat, when Rue appeared at the end of the street.

It was late afternoon, and the sidewalk was empty. The typical rush of commuters parallel-parking badly after a long work day had died down. It was quiet in that way cities are at dusk, the low hum of tires and the distant murmurs of conversation weaving a strange cocoon of stillness. This could have been a nice neighborhood, but the tentacles of gentrification hadn't found it yet.

Gnarled oak trees had heaved and cracked the sidewalk in a dozen places. He'd scared off a raccoon digging through a dented trash can, and there was a shuttered bodega on the corner, the fading posters still advertising cigarettes and booze.

Rue sidestepped a thick root without looking up from her phone despite the horse dog trotting happily at her side. The Great Dane could be a problem, but Griff knew a gentle giant when he saw one. The dog was probably more likely to lick him to death than cause any real damage.

Besides, he didn't plan on alarming her. Not right away, at least.

Griff put on his best smile, the easy, charming one he used on grandmas and unsuspecting girls, but she didn't look up as she passed.

Rue looked different than the first time he saw her. A long gray wool coat swept the tops of scuffed black boots, and a white wire dangled from the headphone secured in one ear. The hoodie underneath her coat was pulled up to cover her dark hair, which escaped from the edges, puffing around her rosy cheeks. She stopped in front of her front door, rummaging in a Trader Joe's tote bag with one hand.

There was nothing remotely magical about her.

She hunched her shoulders against the cold, struggling to open the door while her comically large dog twisted the leash around her knees. Her movements were jerky, and she was muttering like someone who was barely holding it together. Like someone who was at the tail end of a VERY BAD DAY.

Griff knew about bad days. It almost made him reconsider what he was about to—

Snap!

There was only one sound like that. Griff grimaced. Her door key had broken inside the lock. For a lucky girl, she seemed to have more than her share of misfortune.

Griff stepped out of the shadows as the dog looked eagerly between the key stub in Rue fist and the locked door. He expected crying or a stream of swear words, but the girl just tilted her head, staring down at her hand, as if she didn't comprehend what had just happened.

He raised his eyebrows. A shit day came in many forms. It could be catastrophic, taking the horrible shape of a fatal diagnosis or unbearable loss, but the cruelest moments were sometimes the smallest. In his experience, it was the spilled coffee and the burnt dinner that broke people.

He stepped closer to see her profile, catching the pretty flush on her round cheeks and the dimple hidden in the corner of her downturned mouth. She was still staring at the broken key, the dog pressed tight against her hip from his self-imposed short leash. Finally, she turned, the movement oddly stilted, and held up the key as if she had known he was standing there all along.

"It broke," she said matter-of-factly. "Inside the lock."

She was pretty. It wasn't an important fact, but his brain helpfully informed him anyway.

It was impossible not to notice the green of her eyes in the afternoon sun or the lush body hidden underneath the oversized coat. He'd noticed the first time, too, but her hair was softer this time, falling in dark waves around her shoulders, and she had more than a few freckles across her nose.

For the briefest moment, he thought she might ask him for help, but then her spine straightened, and the softness vanished. She stepped back suddenly, glancing down the lonely sidewalk, like any sane woman realizing she was alone with a strange man. Her hand slipped into her coat pocket, and he had no doubt that her thumb was finding the trigger of a can of pepper spray.

The whole thing might have ended there, but then her head tilted. "You," she said, looking confused.

He held up his hands. "I'm not going to hurt you."

This was not entirely true, but she didn't know that.

"I feel like this is the second time we've had this conversation," she noted, glancing down at her phone.

Shit. He was going about this all wrong.

"You're right. That's weird," he said, with a (hopefully) disarming laugh, and introduced himself.

She didn't look any less skeptical after learning his name. "You're here to see Mr. Moretti again, Griff Banks?"

He'd dressed up for the occasion, wearing a deep blue shirt that brought out the hint of color in his smoky eyes, and a tailored coat that hugged his lean frame. He'd trimmed his beard, but kept his curls unruly. Expensive but approachable. It was a look that normally flustered cute girls, which was exactly what he'd been going for.

Rue, however, did not look flustered. Griff hesitated. He'd stalked her on Hinge last night after finding out almost nothing at the shelter.

Her profile was pretty standard for a girl in her late twenties:

ISO a serious relationship.

Likes cooking and the ocean.

Favorite movie: Barbie

Favorite Music: Florence and the Machines

And her profile pic was a cute shot of her sitting on a park bench with the Great Dane.

"Listen, Griff Banks," Rue said, interrupting his thoughts. "I've had a bad day, and I'm going to need some answers, or I'm calling the cops."

She untangled herself from the horse-dog as she said it, adorably spinning in place instead of just unwinding the leash.

"Well, don't do that," he insisted, trying his charming smile one more time.

Rue sighed. She looked tired. Not tired in the I-really-need-to-get-to-bed-earlier type of way. Tired in a lonely way. In a basement apartment way.

Fuck.

"I just...couldn't stop thinking about you," he stammered, running a hand through his hair. "And I didn't know your name."

"So you thought you'd do a doorway jump scare?"

He didn't have to fake his sheepishness. "On further analysis, I could have come up with a better plan."

The horse-dog padded over as she considered, sniffing his boots. He was nervous. As if this were an actual date and not a potential kidnapping.

"I think you should reconsider," he said, giving her his most charming smile. "Going out with me."

She gave him a hint of a smile at that, and he noticed her lips for the first time, full and kissable.

"You have terrible timing," she said, staring down at her broken key. Her hood had fallen back, and her wavy hair puffed around her bunched collar. She had a couple of extra piercings in her left ear.

She was more than pretty, he realized, but it was the kind you had to look for. The kind you notice with your fingertips when a girl is tucked underneath you in the dark or laughing with you—slick and warm—during a morning shower.

Griff discovered he wanted her to say yes for more reasons than one.

"How about this?" he said. "I'll call a locksmith, and we'll grab coffee while we wait for them to fix the door. If you hate me, we can pretend like this never happened. It's the least I can do after being a weird stalker."

Rue studied him for a minute, as the dog wandered over for a pet. Griff complied, giving the beast a healthy scratch behind the ears. She glanced down the sidewalk again, as if someone else (better) might be coming to save her, but there was no one. She sighed. "There's a coffee shop a few blocks down."

Seven

"What do you want?"

Cyan looked annoyed, as usual, as if he were personally offended by the audacity of a customer asking for coffee in a coffee shop. Rue wrapped Tug's leash around her knuckles, keeping him close even though the place was empty.

Griff was parking his car outside. She'd insisted on walking to the Dripolator after their weird encounter at her front door. He was cute, but she wasn't stupid enough to get in the car with a stranger, even with Tugboat at her side.

The man had followed her down the sidewalk in his shiny, expensive car, waving cheerfully every time she looked back at him. Rue sighed. She was really scraping the bottom of the dating barrel these days.

Cyan was staring at her, one finger tapping impatiently. Rue had been hoping for Melody, the barista with the she/they button on her apron, and a true talent for making lavender lattes.

Melody wasn't exactly charming, but at least they weren't rude. The Dripolator had 2.5 stars on Yelp and a half-dozen reviews complaining about the service. It wasn't the sort of café that featured cascading plants or warm lighting or a colorful chalkboard announcing the day's specials. Gritty 90's punk blasted from the speakers—always a little too loudly—and the only sign was a piece of cardboard taped to the back of the espresso machine that announced: NO WiFi--don't fucking ask.

Cyan was perched on a stool, a pink highlighter tucked next to his shaggy mullet. He widened his eyes dramatically at her, rolling his hand in a "come on" gesture that was not HR approved.

"Americano?" she squeaked. It wasn't her drink order, but Cyan always made a disgusted sound in the back of his throat when anyone ordered a flavored coffee (or heaven forbid, something iced). She just couldn't handle one more damn thing, not even the disapproval of a snobby barista.

Cyan grudgingly slipped off his stool, rolling his eyes when she tentatively asked him to leave room for cream.

Annoyed, she glared at the barista's back while he steamed her milk. Timid wasn't her thing, but it had been seeping into her life lately. Self-doubt had put a waver in her voice that she hated.

Maybe *she* was the reason every Hinge date turned out to be a loser, and her chest ached all the time, and she couldn't seem to stick to any-damn-thing, not even to crochet a scarf or—

"Here," Cyan said, sliding a mug across the counter. Coffee splashed over the rim. There was no room for cream.

Ruth left a 20% tip anyway, clocking a table by the windows that looked clean-ish. She should have picked a better date spot, but there were cute couples in cozy cafes. Moms feeding their toddlers tiny pieces of pumpkin bread, and friends meeting over steaming mugs of matcha. There would be laughter in those places, and she'd never felt less like laughing.

"What's his name?"

Ruth paused with the coffee still in her hand, the mug burning her fingers, and looked at Cyan. "What? Who?"

The barista leaned over the counter. "The dog. What's his name?"

She glanced down at the Great Dane, who'd wedged his big head under her elbow. "Oh. This is Tug. As in boat."

Cyan laughed, and Rue tried not to look alarmed when he pulled a dog treat from a Tupperware container on the counter.

"I'm studying to be a vet," he said, leaning over to hold out the treat.

Tug sniffed it daintily, looking up at her for permission. Rue nodded, and he took it, nearly swallowing Cyan's hand in the process. The barista smiled and patted Tug on the head, despite the slobber. Rue blinked at him and then, when it was clear she was being dismissed, made her way to the table and sat.

She'd never considered that Cyan might be a fully formed human with feelings and aspirations, but the thought suddenly made the back of her eyelids hot. Rue wondered if he had someone waiting for him at home. Someone who knew his pizza order and waited to watch the new episode of Severance together.

Even Cyan, the bitchy barista, had a better life than her.

Rue shrugged off her wet coat and adjusted her shirt. It was wrinkled from being at the bottom of her duffel bag for the past few days, but the emerald shade brought out her eyes. There were worse things she could have worn for an impromptu date, but the truth was, it was her last clean shirt.

Thankfully, she'd stopped at the gym this morning to use the shower before Mikey called to say the apartment was finally ready. She'd been feeling sorry for herself, so she'd done a long blowout in between naked grandmas and crying toddlers, and now her hair fell in soft waves around her shoulders. Her makeup was minimal, just blush and gloss thrown on in a scratched locker room mirror, but it would have to do.

Rue took a sip of coffee, wincing at the bitterness as—

Griff swept into the coffeeshop, cold air swirling around him as he flicked down the hood of his coat, shaking rain from his tousled hair. God, she hated dating.

He winked at her and then strode up to the counter, where Cyan was bent over a thick book. After two long beats, the barista gave a dramatic sigh and looked up, blinking when he got a look at Griff.

"Oh, hi. Hey. Um...." Cyan closed his book with a heavy thump. "What, uh, can I get you?"

Griff's eyes flickered over the barista, and he smiled. It wasn't a real smile, though. It was a weapon, finely honed and sharp.

Cyan didn't seem to notice. He slipped off his stool, color rising on his cheeks.

"What's good here?" Griff asked, leaning against the pastry case.

Cyan looked over his shoulder as if there was one of those fancy coffeeshop menus on the wall behind him instead of a ripped poster of David Bowie and a growing water stain. He turned back, looking slightly embarrassed. "Pour over? Ethiopian?"

Griff's weapon widened. "Perfect. How much?"

Cyan let out a nervous little laugh and flapped a hand as if the concept of money was ridiculous, and turned to make the coffee. Stunned, Rue watched as Griff made his way over to her table, pausing to pet Tug before slipping into the chair across from her.

"Did you just flirt with Cyan to get a free coffee?" she hissed.

He leaned back, stretching out his legs. The smile was gone. There was something watchful and dangerous about his face without it. "Yes?"

Underneath the table, Rue pressed a sweaty palm against her thigh, determined to keep it together better than the ruffled barista. "I once saw Cyan make a little kid cry because she asked for marshmallows with her hot chocolate."

Humor touched Griff's gray eyes. "I'm sure he's very nice." His voice dropped an octave. "When he wants to be."

Shit fuck damn, this guy. He clearly knew the effect he had on people and used it to his advantage. She hated men like that.

Rue narrowed her eyes. Her usual first-date questions suddenly seemed stupid. She had no interest in finding out what movies Griff had watched lately.

"Are you into guys?" she heard herself ask.

He shrugged. "I'm into you."

"Not exactly an answer."

Griff gave her the weapon smile and crossed his ankles. The steel tips of his boots were scuffed despite his sophisticated outfit. She wondered what he needed boots like those for and then decided that she probably didn't want to know.

"Griff. I don't usually do this kind of thing."

He sat forward, propping his elbows on the table. She could smell his cologne, something musky with jasmine undertones. A tattoo she hadn't noticed before peeked out of his shirt sleeve.

The corners of Griff's eyes crinkled nicely. "What kind of things don't you do, Rue? Go on dates at shitty coffee shops?"

Maybe it was the arrogant smile or Cyan's frantic energy as he prepared Griff's coffee over at the counter, but she found herself leaning forward too, reaching out to wrap her fingers around his wrist. She turned it over and touched his tattoo.

"Tell me about this," she said softly. His pulse jumped underneath her fingertips.

Griff wasn't smiling anymore. The false charm had drained away at her touch. She liked him better this way.

At the counter, there was the sound of shattering glass, and Cyan swore, but neither of them looked up. Griff's skin was cool to the touch.

"Dragon," he answered, wariness barely masked behind his gray eyes. "Got it when I was eighteen because I thought it would get me laid."

"Did it?" she teased, tracing the dragon's tail with her finger. His eyes flicked to her lips and—

"Ahem."

They jumped apart as Cyan set a steaming to-go cup down between them. "The pour-over broke, so I made you an Americano. We close in fifteen."

He turned on his heel and stalked away. Griff squinted at Cyan's retreating back, rubbing his wrist absently like someone who'd just escaped too-tight handcuffs.

"Maybe you're right about our friendly neighborhood barista."

Rue did not want to talk about Cyan. "What do you do? For a living?"

"Are we really going to do the boring date questions?"

She sipped her coffee and shrugged. "It's standard practice."

He held up his hand, ticking things off on his fingers. "I'm in finance. My favorite color is orange. My last long-term relationship was a year ago, and it ended cause she got a job offer in New York. I like TikTok dogs, horror novels, and good street tacos. My parents are dead, but it was a long time ago, so you don't need to comfort me. My dream travel destination is the coast of Portugal, and I have a pretty badass record collection."

He looked at her expectantly. She liked him, Rue thought. This was already better than her last three Hinge dates, and she'd slept with the last one. Still.

"Orange?" she teased.

"What's wrong with orange?"

"It's a weird favorite color. A red flag if you ask me."

He laughed in that way that made her think of the bedroom. "And what are your red flags, Rue Adler?"

"Oh, I have so many."

"I'm bracing myself."

She tilted her head, pretending to think, and then said, "I like dogs more than humans. My mom is a chronic narcissist. I think pizza is overrated, and Twilight was a pretty good movie. My last relationship lasted three dates, and he ghosted me. I like cheap beer, watching YouTube videos about crafts I'll never do, and fan fiction. Oh, and my favorite color is green."

At the counter, Cyan gathered his stuff loudly, keys jingling. Griff's fingers tapped against his coffee as he studied her, and Rue tried not to hold her breath.

The lights snapped off, plunging the cafe into darkness.

"We're closed," Cyan said into the darkness.

Griff chuckled. "Pizza?"

"There's a little dive bar down the block that serves really good greasy tater tots," she heard herself say.

"Now you're talking. Tots are my favorite food. Especially the greasy kind."

She reached for her coat. "Must be your lucky day."

Even in the darkness, she felt Griff's sudden silence. A vacuum between the banter.

"Do you believe in luck?" his voice asked, far too casually.

Rue froze.

Oh.

A hollow cracked open in her chest. The desire to close her eyes and not wake up until spring was becoming increasingly appealing. Did she believe in luck? Hell yeah. The bad kind.

Griff knew about her. Of course.

This wasn't a date. It was a recon mission. He wanted something.

She should care that he was using her, but for some reason, she couldn't muster up the energy as Cyan bustled them out of the shop. Getting drunk and fucking a fuck boy suddenly seemed like the only good idea left. Rue just hoped she'd feel the same when the bill was due.

Eight

His good luck charm was drunk.

Griff watched Rue flirt with the young man behind the bar, her body half sprawled across the sticky counter to touch his arm. The bartender gave Rue a strained smile and then shot him a not-so-subtle look of desperation over her head.

Griff chuckled, finished off his whisky, and nudged the empty glass across the bar with his knuckle. He wasn't a drinker. Beer was too bitter and heavy, and those fruity cocktails made him feel like he was ordering a Frappuccino at Starbucks. Liquor was simple and impressed rich men, something he needed often.

He stood, sliding a hand around Rue's waist. Their night had started out innocently enough, with a few games of darts and a couple of margaritas, but she'd spiraled into party girl after the third drink.

"I think it's time to get you home," he said. He couldn't help but notice the soft curve of her hip underneath his—

"Griff!" Rue exclaimed, spinning toward him too quickly. She wobbled comically on the barstool before tipping into his arms. He caught her easily, but she pressed against him instead of stepping away. She smiled blearily up at him, her fingers tangling in the hair on the back of his neck. The sensation made his scalp prick.

"I was just going to get this handsome gentleman's number," she pouted, waving at the bartender who was trying to look busy cleaning pint glasses, his wedding ring prominently displayed—not to mention the rainbow flag pin on his apron.

"Unfortunately, I think your prince charming is taken," Griff noted.

Rue blinked, as if seeing the bartender for the first time. Her shoulders sagged. She shook her head. "They always are."

Griff stifled a laugh. "I'm sure you'll meet Mr. Wonderful soon."

He tossed his credit card onto the bar behind her back. Visibly relieved, the bartender took it, flicking off the neon OPEN sign by the window on his way to the register.

"You have pretty eyes," Rue breathed up at him. She smelled like tequila and honey mustard. It shouldn't have been adorable, but it was. "Maybe *you're* my Mr. Wonderful."

Griff rolled his pretty eyes. He suspected that Rue didn't drink frequently. Or pout. She seemed like the kind of girl who chose to live in the world instead of escaping it. Most people used gambling, sex, or drugs to soften the blow. The people who faced it without vice were often the bravest but also the saddest.

Although with Rue's arms around him, reality didn't feel quite so cold.

The bar was just one step above a dive, but the twinkle lights leftover from Christmas gave it a warm glow. The tots and chicken wings hadn't been gourmet, but they'd been freshly fried and dripping with grease. A speaker sat on top of the broken jukebox in the corner, spitting out a mix of Johnny Cash and mournful love ballads. At some point, Rue had decided they were dancing, so she swayed against him in that way only the properly drunk could, her breath warm against his collarbone.

The place was empty, if you didn't count the busboy flicking pool balls across the torn felt table in the back room or the woman in wrinkled scrubs sipping a beer at the end of the counter. The floor had that tacky feeling of never being properly mopped, and the rattling heater wasn't putting off nearly enough heat.

Still, there was the tickle of Rue's hair and the way her fingers clutched the waistband of his jeans. Her shampoo smelled good, something subtle and sweet, and he could feel the slow thud of her heart matching his own.

Griff couldn't remember the last time it had been like this with a girl, soft and quiet. Sex wasn't elusive for him. He went on a respectable number of "dates", but this felt different. This was someone clinging to him as if he were a buoy.

The song changed. Something sad and indie, he recognized but couldn't name.

"Do you ever feel like if you disappeared, no one would notice?" Rue sighed, her voice muffled by his shirt.

Griff let his chin rest on the top of her head. "That can't possibly be true for you."

He meant it. She was pretty and funny and kind. She had a job that she loved and made a difference in this dumpster fire of a world. There must be tons of people who would be worried if she went...missing.

Rue lifted her head, and Griff wished she hadn't. Her eyes shimmered with unshed tears. What color were they anyway? Emerald? Aqua? Some sort of fae witch color?

"It is true," she insisted, worrying her bottom lip with her teeth. Her full, very kissable, bottom lip. Bits of her dark hair clung to her glistening cheeks.

Shit. Fuck.

Griff couldn't help himself.

He kissed her, leaning down to brush away the mark she'd made on her lip with his own. He'd planned it as just a soothing gesture for a sad girl, but Rue sighed and melted against him, and suddenly it wasn't charity at all.

Margarita salt clung to the corner of her mouth. He licked it off, just a quick dart of his tongue. She made a breathy sound, and he found himself gripping her jaw, tilting her head so he could deepen the kiss.

She was warm, moving against him in a way that couldn't be mistaken for dancing. He swallowed his own sound as he tasted her, vaguely aware that they were standing in the middle of a public space.

Her hand came up to cup his cheek. It was a gentle gesture—the kind reserved for boyfriends or lovers, not strangers you made out with in a bar.

Griff pulled away so abruptly that Rue stumbled, and he had to put a hand on her elbow to steady her. The bartender's gaze slid over to them, curious, but Griff gave the man his best charming smile and shrugged in the universal oh-gee-willikers-drunk-girls-am-I-right?

The bartender swirled his index finger in the air in response. It was time to go.

Rue swayed in front of him, staring down at her feet, her brow furrowed in that I-think-I-might-puke realization all tipsy girls get eventually. Her lips were swollen and wet. He wanted to kiss them again.

Griff swallowed and shook off the thought. A nice guy would call an Uber and make sure she got home safe. Would send a text in the morning with a headache emoji and a "nice to meet ya."

But he was not a nice guy. So he helped her into her coat instead and led her out into the falling snow toward his car, where Tug was asleep in the passenger seat.

He wasn't going to hurt her. He wasn't a monster. He was just going to...borrow her.

***

Her bed was moving.

Rue blinked to make sure her eyes were open, wincing at the grittiness behind her lids, but the darkness was complete, which was weird because the cheap blackout curtains in her bedroom usually let in too much light.

Also, the bed was still moving.

She squinted, trying to remember anything about the night before, but it was like digging memories from mud. Her head pounded, a constant whoosh-whoosh between her ears, and she needed to pee. Wherever she was, the mattress was as hard, and the room smelled vaguely like...gasoline?

Rue groaned. Her mouth tasted as if she'd sucked on an old washcloth. The last thing she remembered was the coffee shop? Cyan and his damn americano? There must have been alcohol involved somewhere.

She lifted her hand to rub her forehead, but her elbow clunked against something solid above her. Tentatively, she touched the flat surface that hovered three inches from her nose. Was she in a bunk bed? Jesus, had she fucked someone who still slept in a damn...

The bed bounced violently around her. Her body jerked, nose colliding with the cold metal above her. Tears sprang to her eyes as the car jostled over another bump. Her brain fog cleared instantly.

She was in the trunk of a car.

Oh god.

The whoosh between her ears became a thud.

Thud. **Thud. THUD!**

Rue put up both hands, blindly feeling the underside of the trunk. She was in a metal tomb.

Oh god.

Wide awake now, Rue felt around frantically, her fingers scraping the rough carpet underneath her. She stretched out her feet, finding the end of the trunk with the tip of her boots. Her breath came short and fast. Maybe she was dreaming. Maybe this was one of those nightmares where she woke up, and everything was fine.

Oh god, please be dreaming.

The car turned. She braced herself, banging her knee as she rolled wildly around the trunk. This was real.

The night before flooded back to her.

And Griff. She'd sensed he was dangerous. Not dangerous in the way that made her reach for the pepper spray, but in the handsome way with smoke for eyes and honey for a tongue.

Turned out her instincts were shit. He was definitely pepper-spray dangerous. The smooth talker had bought her tequila and danced with her in the empty bar, and for a second, she'd pretended that it was real. She was definitely the stupidest girl in all the land.

"Shit," Rue muttered, trying to slow her breathing. Now that she was awake, it was ridiculous that she'd ever thought this was a bed, even with a hangover. The trunk was cramped and hard against all her pointy bits.

Griff hadn't seemed like a murderer. Sure, he had those watchful eyes and the dark quietness, but she'd thought he was just one of those moody poet types that liked Bon Iver. Turns out he was the kidnapping type.

"That's on me," she told the darkness.

Rue rolled over, her hip wedging against the underside of the trunk as she explored it. She was hoping for a tire iron, but honestly, she'd settle for anything that could be considered a weapon. She'd seen the same YouTube videos every woman had seen. The ones about knocking out the taillight and waving your hand at passing drivers. Good thing she had no idea how to do that. She wasn't exactly a car expert, and the place where the headlights might be was covered with a panel that required a screwdriver.

NEVER LET THEM TAKE YOU TO A SECOND LOCATION!

The advice was a neon sign in her head, reminding her that she was an idiot.

Her searching fingers finally touched something soft wedged above her head. She squeezed, pulling it closer.

It was a pillow. Weird.

Confused, she discovered that her lower half was covered in a blanket. It was scratchy and smelled like mulch, but it was warm. The kind of blanket you kept in a trunk for emergencies. Double weird.

NEVER LEAVE YOUR DRINK UNCOVERED!

Rue told her brain to shut up. She was fully clothed (thank god) and her debit card and ID were still stuffed into her bra. The only thing missing was her phone. After a little more searching, she found an oddly shaped paper bag, a bottle of water, and something cold and cylindrical that could only be a flashlight.

She switched it on, blinking.

Her situation did not improve with light. The trunk was spacious (for a trunk) and covered in thin gray carpet. There was a bottle of engine oil tucked into one of the cubby's by her feet and a set of jumper cables, but other than that, it was empty. Well, except for the bag of goldfish and the bottle of water.

Rue considered the bottle for a second, but it was clearly sealed. She took a long swig, grimacing at the gross taste in her mouth. Her stomach rolled in time with the moving car, so she munched on a goldfish and considered her very bizarre situation.

What kind of kidnapper made sure you were comfortable before locking you in the trunk? Was this some Hansel and Gretel serial killer shit? Was he gonna fatten her up before boiling her in a big witch's pot?

The car turned abruptly. She gasped, bracing her feet, but the water bottle slammed against her head, and goldfish scattered. The car jolted and bounced, clearly on a dirt road. Her pulse kicked up again. Wherever they were going was close.

If she were smart, she would calculate the time they'd been driving by the estimated speed and come up with some sort of distance, but she had gotten a C in math class. She was looking for another solution when her flashlight caught on something pink stuck to the underside of the trunk.

It was a Post-it note. Two actually.

The first one said (in barely legible boy handwriting), "*I'm sorry.*"

The second one added, "*I'm not going to kill you.*"

"Oh, well, that's a relief," Ruth told the trunk. And, to be honest, it was. Griff didn't seem like a murderer because he wasn't. This was about Luck.

Suddenly, it all made sense: the kiss. The kindness. The booze.

They were breadcrumbs—the trail leading to the cage. Griff hadn't been interested in her at all. He'd wanted something. Her throat tightened, which was ridiculous because she should be a lot more concerned about this kidnapping situation than her pathetic love life.

The car slowed. Rue switched off the flashlight, hefting it in her hand. It was heavy, but she wasn't delusional. It wasn't a great weapon—but it would have to do.

Gravel crunched under the tires. The car stopped. She shifted into a crouch in the tight space and breathed.

Nine

Mistakes had been made.

Griff stared out the windshield, hands gripping the steering wheel as the car idled at the end of his long driveway. It must have been windy last night because drifts had formed on either side of the cabin's covered porch. Dawn was breaking over the roof, and sunlight spilled through the trees, making the snow sparkle.

Tug was curled awkwardly on the seat next to him, long limbs dangling everywhere. He snored when he slept—big, man snores that made Griff laugh, despite the situation.

Griff cut the engine. The dog's dappled gray ears twitched, but he didn't bother lifting his head at their arrival. It would have been a cozy scene if there hadn't been a girl in his trunk.

He rubbed the back of his head and grimaced. She wouldn't understand, of course. No sane person would "understand."

Rue would have forgotten the way she'd become belligerent after leaving the bar, yelling at him about bad luck and one-night stands as she puked in the bushes. She wouldn't remember taking a swing at him for being "too nice" and then sobbing in his arms. She definitely wouldn't remember passing out on the curb beside his car.

In retrospect, he should have put her in the back seat, but he'd been doing some work on the cabin, and there was a bunch of equipment back there. Two crates of tools and a pile of used trim he'd been meaning to drop at the dump.

Besides, the trunk had looked more comfortable. It was the kind of terrible conclusion only reached at 3 am.

Griff rolled down the passenger window before opening his door in case the dog wanted to escape. Tug yawned and stretched.

"Your mom's going to be mad at me," Griff said, patting the dog's butt. Tug huffed in response as if he was well aware of the trouble Griff was in, but didn't bother uncurling from the seat.

Griff sighed and got out, wrapping his coat around himself as a gust of frigid air swept through the thick stand of trees that surrounded the cabin. It smelled like the snow and salt.

Through the forest, the ocean glittered. There weren't many bad things about living in a cabin on a bluff overlooking the Pacific, but the unexpected weather was one of them. It was always a little cold, even in the summer months, and the wind howled like a ghost at night.

Griff stomped his feet, chiding himself for complaining, as he stared at the closed trunk.

His life hadn't always been so lucky. His childhood home had been situated between a rundown Dollar General and the neighborhood crackhouse, but they still had to walk the half a mile to the school bus on dark mornings because his mom worked nights—even when it was so cold that his sister's wet hair froze crispy on the ends.

Still, sometimes the wind sounded like mourning at the cabin, especially on lonely nights.

Griff fiddled with his keys. He was stalling.

Tug was watching him with interest through the rear window, his chin resting on the back of the front seat, ears perked. Griff wasn't uninterested himself. There was no telling what was about to happen.

Rue was probably still unconscious, he told himself. He'd just open the trunk and carry her into the house, tuck her into bed, and make coffee. All would be forgiven.

It was a nice story. Griff pushed the button.

***

Rue launched herself out of the trunk, screaming and wielding the flashlight like a club. She might have successfully made contact with Griff's chin if her foot hadn't caught on the lip of the trunk, causing her to tumble wildly out of the car.

She had only a second to take in Griff's wide eyes and her unfamiliar surroundings before she managed to find her footing. Cabin. Driveway. Woods.

Adrenaline surged through her, and she headed for the trees, but before she could make it more than three steps, Griff grabbed her, wrapping her in a bear hug. He was yelling something, but she couldn't hear him over her own shrieks.

She fought him so hard that he picked her off the snowy ground, staggering backwards a step. Her feet pinwheeled, one heel connecting with his shin. Griff swore in her ear, but didn't loosen his grip.

Frantic, she tried to use her elbows, but he had them pinned and was shushing into her ear like she was an overeager puppy. Fuck him and every man ever born.

Rue slammed her head backward. The crack of his nose echoed inside her skull. He yelped, and she slithered out of his grip, stars dancing in front of her eyes.

She managed three more steps before he caught the tail of her coat. She fell to her knees, gravel biting into her palms, and instinctively kicked backwards, trying to finish the damage she'd done to his nose. He reared back, letting go of her coat. Rue risked a glance over her shoulder as she scrambled forward.

"I'm not going to hurt you!" Griff gasped, blood dripping from his nose and over his bottom lip.

"That's what all the murderers say!"

She crab walked backward, her heels skidding in the loose gravel, in an attempt to put distance between them. Griff put his hands on his knees, his breath a hot plume.

"Shit! I'm sorry!" He shook his head. "I thought you would still be out, and I just needed your help and..."

She threw the flashlight at his head. He ducked, spatters of blood spraying on the muddy snow.

"Rue—stop! Please let me explain."

She did not stop. She was dumb enough to trust a cute guy who showed her a modicum of attention, but at least she wasn't dumb enough to obey shouted commands from a kidnapper. Rue staggered to her feet, one hand out as if she could ward him off with her bleeding palm, but he didn't get up from where he was kneeling in the snow.

"Rue, I...I need your help," Griff begged, still on his knees in the snow. There was blood smeared across the back of his hand.

"And this is how you ask?" she shrieked. She didn't wait for an answer, spinning on her heel and running for the trees.

"I'm sorry!" He called after her, and then, "Be careful!"

Rue didn't bother dignifying that with an answer. She plunged into the woods, branches clasp at her clothes as she ran, slipping over patches of icy leaves, and tripping over bulging roots. It was a typical Oregon forest, wild and untended, with thick underbrush.

"There's a cliff!"

The panic in Griff's voice carried clearly through the trees. Rue skidded to a stop, grabbing at a spindly pine just as the ground dropped away beneath her. She clung to the sapling as dirt bounced down the embankment beyond the toe of her boots. The ocean churned twenty feet below, thick sheets of ice riding the pounding waves before breaking against the shoreline.

She scrambled backwards before collapsing in the underbrush, chest heaving. Her head still pounded from too much tequila, and she'd scraped her knee during her daring escape. It throbbed.

Rue didn't have to turn around to know that Griff hadn't chased her. The white-capped ocean stretched out endlessly toward the horizon, and no other houses lined the shore as far as the eye could see.

Reluctantly, she looked back. Griff's cabin sat on a bluff that was both beautiful and inaccessible to everyone but the privileged. It was modern, despite its rustic style—the kind of house rich people used to pretend they were outdoorsy. The trunk of the sleek sedan was closed now, and Griff was standing beside the passenger door, holding a wad of bloody fast-food napkins against his nose. Tug's head stuck out of the open window and rested on her kidnapper's shoulder.

Griff gave him a friendly scratch while she watched.

Traitor.

"I admit it was a terrible decision to put you in the trunk," Griff called, dabbing at his nose. "I thought you'd sleep until we got here, and I didn't want you waking up and attacking me while I was driving..."

He trailed off. Rue hoped he was hearing his own stupid words.

"Your dog likes me?" Griff said, hopefully.

In response, Tug licked his cheek.

Rue's shoulders sagged. Tug was a lot of things: lazy, lactose intolerant, and a horrible snorer, but he was also an excellent judge of character.

She was in the woods with no phone in the middle of winter, surrounded by the ocean and the endless forest. Best case, she found a road after miles of walking and someone willing to pick up a hitchhiker (who wasn't a murderer). Worst case, she got lost and died out here in the snow with a lovely view.

Rue sighed and started back toward the cabin. Sometimes the best option was the devil you know.

Ten

There was no sign of Griff (or her traitorous dog) when she got back to the driveway, but the cabin's front door had been left open. Her phone was sitting face down on the car's hood like a peace offering.

Rue kept one eye on the house as she crept over to it, in case this was an elaborate trap. Aside from the snow drifts, the front porch was clean. An old wreath still hung from the door, dropping needles onto the welcome mat. It seemed like a good sign. What kind of evil person hung a Christmas wreath?

She picked up her phone, but it was dead (of course). Just once, she could use a little of her own Luck.

Rue tapped it on the hood, idly picking leaves from her hair. She was who-knows-how-many miles from home and wildly hungover. Her stomach lurched with every movement, and the dull pounding between her ears begged for ibuprofen and coffee. No one knew (or cared) where she was, and she desperately needed to charge her phone.

The deciding factor was Tug, who'd disappeared inside Griff's cabin without a smidge of concern for her well-being.

Rue opened the car door. It was spotless, if you didn't count the piles of construction gear taking up the back seat. She'd been on dozens of HInge dates and done her share of kicking aside fast food bags and soda cans in the foot well. She wasn't sure if it meant Griff was a catch or a psychopath.

Considering the last few hours, she was gonna stick with psychopath.

Rue rummaged around inside the car, surprised to find an old pocket knife tucked into the glovebox next to a first aid kit. The blade was approximately two inches long and basically useless, but she felt better holding it. She closed the car door and followed Griff's snowy footsteps into the cabin.

The foyer was rustic but spacious, with wood-paneled walls and a repurposed church pew piled with gloves and scarves. An old-timey beaver hat and a faded red dog leash hung on a coat rack by the door. A heavy oil painting depicting a deep forest in a dozen stunning hues of green was the only decoration.

Griff's boots dripped on the welcome mat. Somehow it made her feel better, as if maybe he would be less dangerous barefoot.

She reluctantly shut the front door, cutting off the swirls of snow blowing around her ankles. Griff didn't appear at the end of the hall with a machete, which she took as a good sign.

Rue palmed the tiny knife and inched down the hallway before stepping into the living room. It was a cavernous space, with a soaring ceiling and a massive antler chandelier. A stone hearth took up one wall, a fire already crackling inside of it. Tug was stretched in front of it at one end of a long leather sectional. He lifted his head when she appeared.

"Are you serious?" she hissed.

He yawned in response, tail thumping. There was no sight of Griff, so she ventured further into the room, halfheartedly checking all the surfaces for a landline as if it were 1998 (no luck).

The back wall was lined with windows overlooking the churning ocean. Opposite the fireplace, the kitchen was just a little too modern for the rest of the decor, as if Griff couldn't help choosing the sleek stainless steel refrigerator and matching chef's stove. A taxidermied black bear guarded the corner, its large paws outstretched and teeth gleaming, which would have been terrifying if it weren't for the Santa hat still perched on its—

Tug barked.

Startled, Rue turned. Tug never barked, and when he did, it was a deep whoof that rumbled in her belly. Usually, it involved the UPS man, but this time he was standing beside the coffee table, long ears dangling as he sniffed the head of a very large potato.

A potato with a puckered scar on its belly.

Rue blinked, staring at the second dog. "Turnip?"

The potato grunted and waddled over to her, stubby tail flapping. She must have stared a second too long because he bumped her shin with his wrinkled forehead, and she unfroze, scooping him into her arms. Tug danced around around them as Turnip slobbered on her neck.

"What are you doing here?" she whispered, pressing her face into the dog's sausage body. His fur was still thin and riddled with scars, but they were healing, and he smelled like shampoo. Turnip farted in response.

She laughed, temporarily forgetting her precarious situation. "Well, it's definitely you. But..."

"Should I apologize again?"

Rue spun, clinging to Turnip with one arm and stabbing the air with the pocket knife. The dog's tiny legs flailed. A few yards away, framed by the hallway entrance, Griff raised an eyebrow at her pitiful weapon. He'd changed into flannel pajama bottoms and a concert tee.

"Did you kidnap Turnip, too?" she demanded.

Griff eyed the dog, who was busy trying to wiggle out of her arms. "I mean, they gave him to me if that's what you're asking. I signed a bunch of paperwork."

Rue glared at him and put Turnip down, dodging licks from Tug. Griff had adopted a dog from *her* shelter. Nice, but also creepy and weird—which seemed to be his specialty.

"How long have you been following me?"

Griff picked up Turnip, holding him like a football under one arm. The dog's tongue lolled happily.

"Did you cyberstalk me before our date?" he countered.

She crossed her arms. "That's different."

(He graduated from Berkeley, his last girlfriend's name had been Liz, and he'd gone on a surfing retreat to Costa Rica last February).

"Tell me what you want or I'm calling the cops," she snapped, trying to ignore the adoring way Turnip was gazing up at Griff. They both knew she was lying. Her phone was very dead, but maybe she'd kick him in the balls and then stab him in the neck and wrestle his phone....

"I don't like the way you're looking at me," he said, crossing the kitchen to a very expensive-looking coffee machine. He set Turnip down on the counter beside it. The dog sniffed the sugar canister. "But you've had a bad night, so I'll let it pass."

She kept the knife aimed at his back while he fiddled with the machine. After a few minutes, the delicious smell of coffee filled the room. Her resolve weakened another notch.

"I'm not helping you," she insisted.

"That's fair. I royally fucked this up." He looked over his shoulder. "You take cream?"

Rue sagged. She was confused, tired, and would slaughter her best friend (if she had one) for coffee right now. Whatever this was about, it was clear Griff wasn't going to hurt her.

She lowered the knife. "Just tell me what this is about."

He opened the cabinet above the machine, revealing an eclectic collection of coffee cups in a rainbow of colors. She'd expected an orderly line of boring white mugs. This man was nothing if not unpredictable.

"I have a business proposition for you," he said, pouring the coffee.

"Do you start all of your business meetings like this?" she responded, watching him add cream and sugar to a mug with a Waffle House logo. "With a kidnapping?"

Griff plopped Turnip back on the ground and grabbed his coffee. He gave her a wide berth before taking a seat on the other side of the kitchen island. He left her mug steaming on the counter. She eyed him suspiciously before crossing to take a sip, and then had to resist the urge to close her eyes at the taste.

The dogs had discovered a lamb chop toy, and the room was filled with squeaks and playful growls. Griff ignored it as if having an MMA fight in his living room was completely normal.

He waited until she took another drink before saying, "I need your...talents. To win a poker game."

She glanced around the huge cabin. "You seem to be doing just fine for yourself. What more could you possibly need?"

It was a dumb question. There was never enough money, especially for those who already had lots of it.

Griff's eyes slipped from hers. "Let's just say it's a game I can't afford to lose."

He was lying. Rue knew it as well as she knew that Griff's coffee beans came from a single source in Guatemala and cost forty bucks a pound, which is to say it was a pretty good bet.

"There are some English muffins and other breakfast stuff in that cabinet," he said, pointing at the pantry behind her. "Pop-Tarts, maybe. Help yourself."

It was a clear distraction, but she was starving, so she dug around for a minute before settling on making a couple of slices of raisin toast. The dogs abandoned their toy and stood at her feet attentively while she spread peanut butter and added sliced banana. Griff watched silently as she gave Tug a piece of fruit and let Turnip lick the butter knife.

"What's in it for me?" Rue asked. "Aside from not being kidnapped."

Griff had the decency to look guilty. "I'll split the winnings with you."

Rue was suddenly painfully aware of her Target-brand clothes and $14 Sheer Cut haircut. Money wasn't something she usually cared about, but it was hard to be poor in a kitchen with gleaming granite and a view of the ocean.

She spotted a charger on the counter and plugged in her phone, waiting until the startup screen blinked on. Griff didn't stop her.

"Why would you do that?" she asked. "You have me already."

"I'm a nice guy?"

"Are you?"

He was quiet, one finger running around the rim of his mug. "I used to be."

Rue studied him, but he kept his eyes off hers. She wasn't a psychic, so his real motivation was a mystery, but she'd dealt with a lot of people who believed money would buy them happiness. And it did—she wasn't naive enough to think otherwise—but money couldn't always fix what was broken. It was a band-aid, not medicine.

Her phone screen blinked to life. Despite being kidnapped the night before, she only had one unread message and no phone calls.

Rue tapped the notification, hoping at least someone was checking to see if she was okay, but it was from her dentist wanting to confirm an appointment next week.

Rue looked up at Griff. "How much?"

He shrugged. "Depends on the game, but probably around 3 million."

Her eyes widened. "Total?"

"No. That would be your cut."

Rue didn't have to think long. "I'm in."

***

"Have you lost your mind?" David screeched.

Rue sat on the steps to Griff's cabin and scratched Turnip's head, one ear pressed to her phone as she watched snow melt from the trees. Her butt was cold and wet, but the rest of her was disheveled from running through the woods and passing out in a trunk, so it didn't matter.

To his credit, David had stayed quiet while she filled him in on what had happened the night before. She'd even skimmed over the kidnapping part, but now, apparently, he had things to say.

"Let me get this straight," he said. "This stranger you met in the STAIRWELL OF YOUR APARTMENT in the MIDDLE OF THE NIGHT asks you on a date—"

"Handsome," Rue interjected.

David paused. She could practically hear his teeth grinding over the phone. "I'm sorry, what?"

"Handsome stranger?" she hedged.

"Girl."

She sighed and waved a hand he couldn't see. "Please, continue with your friendly browbeating."

So he did, ranting about her terrible choice in men (he wasn't wrong) and the dangers of being desperate (strike two) before finishing with, "And now you've decided to HELP HIM?"

"David, you're yelling."

He huffed. "Sorry. I'm just worried about you."

She might have been mad if she hadn't yelled at David numerous times about his own poor dating choices, going so far as following him to work a few times to make sure he didn't go home with whichever asshole he was currently convinced was the love of his life.

She missed him. It had been nice to have someone who cared if she lived or died. On the other end of the phone, David sighed.

Rue watched Turnip hop down the stairs like a loose basketball, trying to come up with a convincing argument for her recent choices.

"He has a really nice smile?" she said lamely.

"Cool story, babe."

It was late afternoon, and David was filming. Over the static, she could hear the sounds of a working sound studio, not that she'd ever been on an active set. She imagined him sitting outside the makeup trailer underneath an LA blue sky, listening to her saga. It seemed so much more glamorous than her own disaster of a life.

"You don't have to help everyone, Rue," David said finally.

It was a loaded statement. They were both aware that her Luck was why David was in California. That it was her Luck that had gotten him his dream job. She wasn't mad about it. It was a natural consequence of being her friend. It just happened to be one that sucked for her.

David had stayed longer than most, though, and she didn't want him to feel guilty, so she decided to tell the truth. "It's good money, David."

"So get a lotto ticket!" he burst out, then swore underneath his breath. "There is no need to put yourself in danger."

"You know it's not that simple." Rue had spent a lifetime avoiding the IRS—repeatedly winning piles of money wasn't something that went unnoticed. Or unpunished.

David went silent. On the other end of the line, someone called his name.

Turnip sniffed one of Griff's tires before lifting his leg to pee. The scar on his belly had faded from angry red to a puckered pink. He was unrecognizable from the day she'd found him tied to the shelter's back door with a frayed piece of rope, his stomach bloody and gasping for breath. It was amazing what love could do.

The bulldog trotted back to her, hopping up the stairs with unusual enthusiasm before plopping next to her. His body was heavy and warm against her thigh.

"He adopted one of my dogs," Rue told the silence.

Nine hundred miles away, David sighed. "That's a long way to go to impress a date."

Rue smiled. "Yeah."

Eleven

The silver-gray stairs that clung to the bluff beside the cabin were slick from ocean mist and algae. He'd been meaning to power wash them for the past few years, but the job was time-consuming and harrowing, so Griff kept one hand on the railing as he descended, occasionally stopping to shoo away a seagull and sidestep broken treads.

A bitter wind blew off the ocean, blasting him with salt and sand. The stairs creaked and groaned under his bare feet. Griff shivered, his wetsuit pulled up just enough to cover his swimtrunks, exposing his chest. The rest of the suit dangled behind him, slapping his heels. He dodged bird shit, and attempted to reconsider his choice of hobbies.

He should take up video games or puzzles, for fuck sake. Anything that kept him inside by the fire in January instead of clinging half-naked on the side of a cliff. This was the worst part of cold-weather surfing—the moments before the adrenaline warmed him, and he sat sweating underneath his neoprene watching the horizon for the next set.

It was 42 degrees today, which wasn't bad for winter in the Pacific Northwest. However, the water wouldn't be much warmer—a sure recipe for hyperthermia without a wetsuit—although it wasn't quite cold enough to turn his hair to ice. Still, the sky was blue above the lingering fog, and soon the sun would at least pretend to warm his shoulders.

Griff's feet sank into the cold sand. High tide lapped near the bottom step, and the roar of the ocean echoed off the rock walls of the cove, but the break was farther out, crashing against an invisible reef.

He'd be lying if he said that break wasn't why he built his house on this particular cliff. All beaches were public land, but the only way to access this tiny cove was by boat or the creaky stairs behind him. This small section of the wild ocean was his, and she was the most fun in the deep winter. Griff wrestled his board from the shed he'd built underneath the stairs, still shivering, and set it in the wet sand.

Griff knelt and added a layer of fresh wax to the surface. He probably should have stayed up at the house with his guest. That would have been the polite, normal thing to do, but the ocean had been calling to him from every window, as if it could sense the fear fizzling underneath his skin.

He hadn't expected Rue to agree to his crazy scheme after the "kidnapping" disaster. Or that she'd want to stay overnight, saying she needed to "get up to speed" on poker as if he could show her how to play a game in one evening that he'd taken a decade to master.

Griff huffed a laugh, stashing the wax back in the shed. She was a piece of work.

He wrestled his wetsuit up over his shoulders, sucking in his stomach to zip it up to his chin. The hood was tight, pulling at the hair around his ears. He wrestled on a pair of wetsuit booties before hoisting the board. It was not the most attractive outfit, but it did the job.

He headed into the surf, gasping when the frigid water splashed on his exposed skin, but after catching a few waves, he was warm enough. The sun had burned off the fog, gilding the edges of the waves with gold. Gulls circled overhead, yelling at each other as they dove for their dinner. At one point, he saw a whale, its massive spine arching above the waves as it migrated down the coast, singing its melancholy song.

Griff never looked back at the beach or the house while he surfed. He liked to pretend, just for a moment, that he was just another animal, small in a huge, wild world. Eventually, he had to straddle the board to rest, heart pounding in time as he studied the waves on the horizon. The tide was turning, and the incoming sets were gentle and less frequent.

The fear was gone, burned away by the sun and sand.

He could have sat there forever, lifting and falling with the breath of the ocean, salt water stinging his eyes, but the sun hadn't chased away enough of the cold. It would only take a few minutes for his calf muscles to lock up at this temperature. Reluctantly, he swung the board back to shore and—

Rue was standing on the beach.

Or he guessed it was Rue, although he could barely tell from the way she was bundled inside the comforter that she must have pulled off the guest bed and dragged down three flights of wet stairs. She was huddled next to the shed, out of the worst of the wind, waiting for him. Griff started to paddle.

***

"Are you crazy?" Griff asked, yanking off the wetsuit's hood and shaking salt water from his hair.

Rue had sunk into the sand, and she peered up at him from her blanket cocoon, no doubt unaware that the Ralph Lauren comforter she was currently ruining had cost a fortune. It did look cozy wrapped around her, though, even with the damp, sandy edges.

He was already shivering, his nose hairs crisping in the frigid air.

"You're the second person to say that to me this morning," she said, laughing. "And I was going to ask you the same thing."

An arm appeared from underneath her blanket. She held something up to him. He took it between two fingers, stretching so as not to drip cold sea water on her.

It was his beanie. The wool one he kept on a hook by the back door and had forgotten to grab before heading out. Something tweaked inside his chest as he planted it on his soggy head.

"Thanks," he grunted. He suspected it made him look like a shipwrecked sailor, but he was instantly warmer.

"Do you always surf in subzero temperatures?" Rue asked as he stowed his board in the shed. Cold water dripped down his back, and he had to clench his jaw to keep his teeth from chattering.

On a typical day, he would already be racing up the steps to keep his blood pumping, so he could strip off the wetsuit and jump in the hot shower before freezing to death, but Rue made no move to stand.

"Only when I'm on the West Coast, and it's winter. Besides, the water is well above freezing today."

He shivered as she got to her feet, looking like a blob with a wedding train. Oblivious to her ridiculousness, Rue tilted her face to the wavering winter sun. Her homemade comforter hood fell to her shoulders, and she closed her eyes as if she were basking in the Bahamas instead of being battered by icy wind.

"Not very safe—surfing alone like that," she told the sun.

Griff was only half listening now, despite the cold. The afternoon light highlighted the bits of gold in her dark hair and the faint freckles that peppered the bridge of her nose. He wondered what it was doing to the shade of her eyes, but she still had them closed.

"I'm touched by your concern," he teased, and part of him meant it. He couldn't remember the last time someone gave a shit if he lived or died.

Rue snorted and rummaged around inside her cocoon before one hand emerged holding a battered travel mug. "Thought you might want something to warm up."

Bottle-green and luminous. That's what the sunlight did to her eyes.

Distracted, he must have stared at the thermos too long because she gave it a tiny shake as if to say, "Yeah, that's for you."

He took it, making sure to touch her as he did. The deep roast-y scent of coffee mixed with the brine of the sea was probably the best thing he'd ever smelled, aside from her hair, maybe.

Griff took a sip. It was piping hot and just how he liked it—sweet and creamy. It warmed him straight to his toes.

"Thanks," he said, licking a stray drop from his lip.

Those bottle-green eyes followed his tongue and then flicked up to meet his gaze. She blushed, and Griff felt his insides heat in a totally different way.

What was he doing? This girl had done nothing but help him out, and here he was thinking about all the ways he could—

He cleared his throat. "I'm surprised you came all the way down here."

She smiled and shrugged. His traitorous mind was wondering what she would say if he invited her to join him in his post-surf shower. If the curve of her naked shoulder also had freckles, and what it would taste like if he—

"I love the ocean," Rue said softly, interrupting his salacious thoughts. She stared out at the waves as the wind tore at her hair, as if that was answer enough.

And it was. The ocean was the only place he felt at peace, and Griff understood being drawn to something.

Or someone.

Twelve

"We're always lucky,' I said, and like a fool, I did not knock on wood." —Ernest Hemingway

R ue didn't expect learning poker to be so funny. Or to get so pleasantly tipsy. But Griff had topped off her drink so many times she'd lost count, tipping the amber liquid into the fancy crystal glasses as if it were water, first on the rocks and later, when they both stopped caring, straight up.

At the beginning of the night, when they were still eating greasy pizza slices from the box, and she was studiously taking notes on poker lingo, he'd mentioned how this particular bottle of whiskey was expensive and rare. At first, it had tasted like rocket fuel to her, but now it went down smooth as smoke.

"That is a terrible hand," Griff observed when she triumphantly slapped down a pair of threes.

He was leaning back in his chair like a teenager, two legs off the floor, and he'd been chewing on a toothpick for the last hour, rolling it from one corner of his mouth to the other in an incredibly distracting way.

Rue knew it was a terrible hand, but she'd mentally changed the stakes of the game hours ago without telling him. Those loose, easy smiles that appear on Griff's face were a better prize than a pile of plastic chips anyway. Brackets framed his mouth, and she had decided she wanted to kiss them—just a light little brush to see if they would deepen, which was a distracting thought and stupid, and definitely the alcohol.

Griff fanned out his cards—a full house.

"This is not a fair fight," she teased. "You're using my Luck against me."

He didn't respond to that, holding up the near-empty whisky bottle and lifting one eyebrow in question. It was well past midnight, and her ass ached from sitting so long in the hard dining room chair. They had an important night ahead of them tomorrow, but neither of them seemed to want to be the first one to head to bed. Turnip and Tug had turned in hours ago, curling up together on the rug in front of the fire, which had burned down to glowing embers.

Still, she nodded, and he splashed the rest of the whisky into their glasses. Rue drank it in one gulp, trying to be satisfied with the warmth of the alcohol instead of a body pressed against her own.

Rue knew he'd happily take her to bed if she asked, and she wasn't quite sure what made her stay silent. It definitely wasn't the way his long fingers shuffled the cards. Maybe it was just dignity.

"So what's it like? Being a lucky charm?" Griff asked while he dealt her cards.

It was a casual question, but it sobered her immediately. Eventually, everyone asked. It was a hazard of being a talisman instead of a person, but, for some reason, it bothered her more tonight.

She tapped her empty glass on the table and considered giving her usual flippant answer. A soft, easy version that absolved people from their own avarice. Not everyone who came to her on their knees was greedy. Most were just good people drowning in the suffering of being a human.

Those were the worst—the ones she couldn't turn away, no matter what it cost her.

Rue peeked at her cards. Pocket Queens. She watched him check his own hand, but there was nothing on his face that could be considered a tell. He caught her looking and winked.

"It's terrible," she said, surprising herself. She shrugged, and it was a lie. "Being lucky has ruined my life."

Griff, to his credit, didn't flinch. He tapped the corner of his cards, head tilted. "Tell me."

She shook her head, wishing she hadn't gulped her last bit of whiskey. "It always starts the same. Just a nice date. A new friend. We hang out a few times, and it's normal, you know—sometimes good, sometimes bad. How it should be."

"But then?" Griff asked. In the fading firelight, his eyes were the color of burnt coals, soft and gray.

"Then they find out. Put it together by accident or a deep internet search." She shrugged, looking away from those soft eyes. " And then everything changes."

"How?"

"They start looking at me like a tool instead of a person."

***

Griff studied himself in the steamy bathroom mirror as he rolled up the sleeves of his shirt. It was couture, no doubt hand-stitched by some nervous intern behind a Tom Ford runway curtain. The buttery gray fabric was light, perfectly tailored, and brought out the smoke in his eyes.

It had taken three cups of coffee and a shower to chase away the hangover from the night before, but his head was finally clear. There was nothing he could do about the shadows underneath his eyes, but he took a breath and smoothed away the worry lines between his brows. He needed to be steady tonight.

Griff reached for the vintage Rolex he wore when he wanted to look wealthy. The black leather strap was cracked from age, and the quartz face was scratched. It cost him 40k in a backroom boutique in Paris. It was like putting on armor.

Wearing the right clothes usually worked to calm his nerves before a high-stakes game, but today he couldn't stop seeing the liar looking back at him in the mirror. He doubted anyone else would notice the poor kid underneath the designer outfit. The one who wore his cousin's hand-me-downs to school and ate peanut butter sandwiches on Fridays instead of the cafeteria's pepperoni pizza because his lunch account was empty.

His mom had worked hard to keep him and his sister clean and fed, pulling 16-hour shifts at the paper factory and coming home with the stink of the place caught in her hair.

Ten-year-old Griff had been resentful that he couldn't have the latest video game release. Fifteen-year-old him had gotten a job so his sister's Christmas stocking wouldn't be empty. Seventeen-year-old Griff had watched his mom die of breast cancer the same year she retired from the factory, the unused postcards of Malibu and the Greek islands still pinned to the inside of her closet door.

The day he picked up his mom's ashes in a cardboard box, Griff had sworn he would find a way to live a life that didn't break him.

He braced his hands on the edges of the sink and checked his appearance one last time. His hair was neat, and the lines of his short beard crisp. He looked wealthy and confident. Not at all like he had to puke. Or that his deodorant might fail before he even left the house.

Griff glanced down at his phone. He'd made six calls this morning and sent over a dozen texts, none of which were answered.

He stepped out of the bathroom and punched her number one more time, listening to the familiar ring. It cut short and then, "Damn it, Griff. Stop fucking calling me."

He straightened. She hadn't answered in weeks. He'd assumed she'd blocked his number. "Sarah—don't hang up."

"Fuck you."

She was whispering, the sound muffled as if she was cupping her hand over the phone receiver. He didn't miss the slur in her words, even though it was barely 5 pm.

Griff searched for any words that weren't begging, but now that he was finally talking to her, his mind went blank. "Please let me help you."

"I don't need your help," Sarah hissed. "I'm fine. Better than fine, Griffin. Happy!"

This was a lie. He knew what happy sounded like, and this definitely wasn't it. He gripped the phone harder. The bitterness of taking care of someone who didn't want to be taken care of was sharp.

"Listen," he said, sitting down on the edge of the bed. "Come home. We'll work it out."

There was a beat of silence, as if she was actually considering it, and then a new voice came from the background—a male voice. The phone muffled as Sarah held it against her chest. He strained to hear her response, but then she was back.

"Griff, I don't..." She sighed. "I don't have a home."

The defeat in her voice was worse than any anger. He pressed the phone closer to his ear. "*This* is your home."

It wasn't. It was barely *his* home.

There was a beat of silence. And then another. Followed by a hollow—**click**.

Griff stared down at the phone, his chest hollow. The call time had been 2 minutes and 32 seconds. Not nearly enough time to make a case. Impulsively, he hit her number again, but this time it went straight to voicemail. His shoulders sagged. She'd finally blocked him.

"You okay?"

Startled, Griff looked up. Rue was framed in the doorway, shifting nervously on bare feet.

She was wearing the outfit he'd had overnighted from one of the exclusive fashion houses in New York. He'd guessed her measurements, but the shimmering silk skirt draped beautifully over her full hips and down to her ankles. The cashmere sweater he'd chosen was purposely loose and fell off one shoulder, giving him a tantalizing view of her collarbone. The entire outfit was deep emerald, gorgeous against her pale skin.

"Is this okay?" she asked, tugging on the skirt as if she didn't look like she had walked right off a runway.

Not short enough, Griff thought instinctively, wondering if the skin on the inside of her thighs was as smooth as the silk of the skirt. Out loud, he said, "You look stunning."

She smiled nervously, scratching the back of her calf with her toes. They were painted coral pink. Griff wished he hadn't noticed.

"I've got some shoes for you somewhere," he said, turning to search through the boxes scattered on the top of his bed so he didn't have to look at her anymore.

"Who were you talking to?" she asked, wandering into the room.

"My sister," he responded, and then wondered why he didn't lie.

Rue picked up a pair of cufflinks from his dresser and then put them down before studying the framed photo of him surfing in Portugal three summers ago. She'd done something to her hair, turning the frizz into silky waves that she'd pinned up on one side with a sparkly clip. The rest fell down her back, the setting sun outside highlighting the glimmers of gold in the rich brown.

Rue picked up another frame and then held it out to him. It was a crayon drawing Sarah had made in kindergarten. "A little sister, I assume?"

She shouldn't be here. Not in his bedroom, with despair roiling in his stomach and that sweet, shy smile. Suddenly, all he could think about was the sound she'd make if he lifted her onto that dresser and slid his hands up her thighs.

"Griff?"

"Here," he replied, thrusting a shoebox in her direction. "These should work."

They should do much more than work. They were 8k-dollar kitten-heel Milanos in a subtle gold finish.

Rue put down the frame and walked over, standing way too close. She was wearing perfume, something subtle and floral that made him lightheaded, and when she looked up at him, her bottle-green eyes framed by soft liner. A faint shimmer highlighted her cheeks. She smiled, her lips glossy, and it was almost his undoing.

"I'm an only child," she said softly. "Always thought it would be cool to have a sibling to play with."

Her dark hair fell in her face as she took the shoe box. He itched to brush it aside. "It's not all it's cracked up to be."

One smooth shoulder lifted and fell. "Neither is loneliness."

Thirteen

Rue had never been to a high-stakes poker game. Hell, she'd never even bought a scratch-off ticket. Luck had never belonged to her in that way.

She'd always imagined that these games took place in a secret room in the back of a ritzy casino filled with exotic sex workers and men with heavy gold rings. She'd imagined expensive drinks and stacks of money and, for some reason, Leonardo DiCaprio dressed as a mob boss.

She *hadn't* pictured a private home with a heavy iron gate that slowly swung open in the headlights of Griff's sleek BMW. The house at the end of the long driveway was a modern monolith, tucked into a dark tree line. It managed to be both sprawling and oddly modest, as if it were embarrassed to be worth a kajillion dollars. The siding was black with accents of rich wood, including the vast ceiling of the portico, where a quiet man in a suit whisked away

Griff's car, promising to keep an eye on Tug, who was napping in the back seat.

Warm lights lit the stone path as they approached, and the bushes on either side of the heavy mahogany door were carefully manicured. It was almost enough to make her forget the red-eye glow of the camera hidden in the eaves.

Rue tried not to fidget as Griff rang the doorbell, even though they obviously knew there were guests on the property. His hand rested lightly on the small of her back as they waited. She wasn't sure if he was being polite or trying to keep her from running away.

She took a nervous breath, trying to look as poised as the man beside her. Griff had swapped his pajamas for tailored dress pants and a soft gray button-down, casual but elegant. It was the kind of outfit that screamed old wealth right down to the Italian loafers and vintage Rolex dangling from his wrist like an afterthought.

He slipped his other hand into his pocket, rocking back on his heels. She tugged at the waistband of her gorgeous skirt, even though it fit as if it had been tailored for her body. Rue was half convinced Griff had also kidnapped a tailor and was keeping them in the basement.

She shifted, adjusting her bra strap.

Griff's gaze finally slid over to her. "Stop fidgeting. Lift your chin. Take a breath. They will eat any sign of weakness as if it's a canapé."

Rue glared at his profile and then did as she was told, straightening her shoulders. She could already feel a blister forming on the back of her left heel from the ridiculous shoes, but three million dollars was a lot of money.

Besides, she could see Griff's hands clenched inside his pocket. She wasn't the only one who was nervous.

"Who the hell says canapé?" she whispered, glancing up at the glowing red eye.

"People who don't eat pizza pockets for breakfast."

Rude. And accurate.

She was preparing a retort when the door swung open, and a statuesque woman wearing a slinky black dress ushered them inside. She did not smile.

Rue tried not to gape at the soaring mahogany ceiling or the koi pond embedded into the wood floor beside a tastful waterfeature. The walls were a deep green, and what looked like an original Monet hung casually over a marble entry table.

"Welcome," said the statuesque woman. She had a thick Slavic accent, and her voice was breathy, as if she were inviting them into her bed rather than to a poker game. "I am Katia, your host for this evening's event. I trust you are aware of the rules?"

Griff nodded, shoulders relaxed. "No weapons. Cash. I already signed the NDA and had it sent over."

"You will let Giovanni check, yes?" Katia's lips smiled, but everything else on her beautiful face stayed in place.

A man stepped out of a side hallway. He wasn't big or burly like a cliche bodyguard, but there was something in the cut of his shoulders that hinted at violence—the cold and calculating kind that didn't have any trouble sleeping at night. Rue stood still as he searched her. His big hands swept over her shoulders and hips before sliding up her thighs, lifting the hem of her skirt enough to make Griff's jaw clench, but she shook her head, warning him off.

The bodyguards' movements were intimate but efficient. She didn't know shit about poker, but she knew about power, and it did not like to be challenged.

After the pat down, Katia led them down the long hallway, her Louboutins clicking loudly on the gleaming wood floor. She did not make small talk. The goon followed uncomfortably close as if he expected them to bolt.

Rue tried not to wobble on her own heels as they went deeper into the house. The back of Griff's hand brushed hers, but he stopped short of taking it. She wasn't sure if she was relieved or disappointed.

Katia ushered them into a surprisingly cozy room at the end of a long hall that could only be described as a wealthy man's man cave. Two men and a woman were seated at a black felt poker table nestled between a full bar and a crackling fireplace. The room was undeniably masculine with dark wood finishes and crystal whisky glasses. It smelled like leather and money.

The older woman at the table was the only hint of femininity, if you didn't count the young bartender. She looked as if she had been ripped from her suite at the Kentucky Derby in perfectly coiffed silver hair and a crisp teal pantsuit.

One of the men stood, coming forward in that confident way only a rich man could manage. "Griff, my good man!"

Rue had expected a fat man with a cigar and a whore on his lap, but the man shaking Griff's hand was in his mid-30s and fit. Grant Reddington's voice was cultured as if he wintered in the Swiss Alps, but he was also tan enough to have a vacation home in the Maldives.

He looked vaguely familiar. Rue guessed he was a CEO of something slimy—either Pharma or oil. He had the distinct look of someone whose wealth was born of the blood of others. She'd probably seen him on CNN.

"And who is this lovely creature?" Grant asked, turning his dazzling smile her way. "My god, your eyes are exquisite!"

The man's charisma was an assault, and she couldn't help but wonder what kind of evil deeds had been ordered through those perfect veneers. She held out her hand politely, careful to keep her wrist loose as she introduced herself. He bowed forward and kissed the back of her hand. She willed her face not to get the ick.

"What can I get you to drink, Ms. Adler? A Cosmo?"

She wrinkled her nose internally. A Cosmo? Really? What was it 2011? Out loud, she said, "That would be lovely."

Grant, the CEO, laughed even though there wasn't anything remotely funny, lifting a finger to the bartender as if she wasn't watching them from three feet away.

The girl just nodded and reached for a glass. She was pretty underneath her bleached hair and smudged mascara, although she barely looked old enough to drink herself, let alone tend bar. Her wrinkled apron looked ridiculous over an incredibly short red sequined dress, and the nametag hanging from it said, "Candi."

There was something about the way she scooped ice—blue eyes wide, cheeks pink, that radiated barely contained anger.

Grant's gaze lingered on the unsmiling girl as if cataloging a rebuke to administer later, but then he turned to Griff, slapping him on the shoulder in that boisterous way men do when they are trying to make sure the lesser man knows who's in charge.

"Your girlfriend is beautiful, Griff. Where did you find her?"

Rue bristled. Who did this asshole think he—

Griff's hand slithered around her waist. Startled, she looked up, but his mouth was already slanting across hers.

She knew it might be coming. Girlfriend was the cover story they'd talked about, but she gasped, and he swallowed her surprise, his fingers tightening in warning on the small of her back.

Rue tried to sink into it, her hand coming up to his chest, but she was no actress. And it was no normal kiss. It was possession.

Everything about the performance was rough except his lips, which were soft and searching on hers. Rue tried to find her indignation, but oh god, his tongue feathered along the bottom of her lip and—

Griff pulled away suddenly, not even glancing down when she wobbled beside him. He looked at Grant instead and smiled a smile that was not a smile. "Don't even think about it, my friend."

The bartender had stopped making the drinks to gape at them. The CEO's eyes narrowed, but one edge of his mouth twitched. "We'll see then, shall we?"

Griff gave a curt nod. Rue's stomach twisted, fear washing the heat from her cheeks. This wasn't the time for swooning. These were dangerous men. The kind that took what they wanted and didn't look back.

They took their seats. No one at the table shook her hand or asked her name as the pretty bartender delivered their drinks. Here she was an object. At best, a lucky charm. A talisman.

At worst, just a woman.

Fourteen

"What's true of the poker game is true of life. Most people are suckers and don't realize it" —Michael Faust

E very poker game has a patsy; usually someone filled with un-
earned arrogance. Someone who has misjudged their talent or is too rich to care. Most people think poker is a game of chance, inherent skill, or years of experience, but it's actually as simple as not being the weakest link.

Griff knew why he'd been invited to this particular game. He'd lost thousands convincing the poker world that *he* was a patsy. It had taken months of losing big. His bets quietly grew more desperate, and the rumors that he was washed up got louder. Soon, some of his opponents had stopped shaking his hand as if bad luck was something that could rub off on their skin.

All of it had led up to this moment.

Griff watched Grant consider his cards, knee pressed against Rue's to keep her from fidgeting. They'd been at it for hours.

The stack of chips in front of Grant made him want to break into a cold sweat, so he concentrated on Rue—the smell of her lilac shampoo and the small sound she made whenever he lost a hand. On a typical day, she would have been distracting, but tonight another woman had that honor.

He hadn't looked up when the bartender had slammed his drink on the table, the alcohol splashing over her knuckles. The girl's name tag said, "Candi." Grant had frowned briefly as she stalked back to the bar, but he had more important things to worry about than a misbehaving employee, and the moment was forgotten.

Griff considered his cards and then bet, tossing 20k into the middle of the table, but Grant didn't so much as flinch before matching it, his chips clattering on black velvet before he flipped the river card—a king of hearts.

It was a solid card considering the trio of hearts in Griff's hand. He flicked his eyes around the table, making sure everyone noticed his nervous shifting. The other three players hadn't been introduced, but he'd done his homework. The handsome man who'd folded first was Manoj Khan, a Bollywood star worth around eight hundred million. The older woman dripping with diamonds was old money, and the oil baron with surprisingly bad teeth had won his billions in Texas.

Griff checked his cards for the third time as the woman folded, pushing her seat back, and gathering her Hermes purse. He nodded politely, but she didn't bother to acknowledge him as she breezed away on a cloud of too-strong perfume.

"That seems good, right?" Rue whispered, her lips brushing his ear. Griff had expected her to lose interest, but she was still watching the game intently, nursing her ridiculous pink drink.

"That is indeed good, little lady," Grant boomed, upping the bet and leaning back. If the man had a beer gut, he would have folded his hands over it in triumph, but he had 6-pack abs, which was even more annoying.

Griff eyed the chips in the center of the table. The pot was up to nearly 250k.

Rue made a small sound next to him at the sight—a mew of disappointment that made his brain think of things that had nothing to do with cards. Griff mentally shook off the distraction. His pulse was a steady thud between his ears. He had the potential for a straight in his hands. It was now or never.

"I'm all in," Griff said quietly, pushing his chips into the middle of the table.

It was a reckless bet. Grant cracked for the first time, his brows furrowing for a moment before smoothing back out. He didn't have enough to match the bet. His lips pursed and he tapped a finger on the table, before asking, "What do you want?"

Griff put a hand on Rue's thigh. He could feel her breathing. His good luck charm. His talisman.

"I'll take the bartender," he said smoothly.

Rue stiffened. At the bar, a glass broke, but Griff didn't bother turning to look at his little sister.

***

Sarah Banks had been trying to figure out how to get her fucking brother to leave without causing a scene since the second he'd waltz into Grant's poker den. She should have known he'd pull something like this after she blocked his number; she just hadn't expected it to happen so quickly.

He was always trying to be a damn superhero as if this shitty existence were something you could be rescued from.

For the first couple of hours, she'd seethed at the back of his head, scooping nugget ice into crystal glasses too loudly and slamming expensive liquor bottles on the bar so hard she was sure they'd shatter.

Still, Griff hadn't bothered to look at her once, not even when he ordered his pretentious ass whisky from her. She's switched it for the cheap stuff that tasted like motor oil, of course, but eventually she had to stop making a racket, since all it did was earn glares from Grant, and tight-lipped disappointment from that Katia bitch who'd already been threatening to fire her for months.

So she waited, furious, while Griff lost all his money.

Her brother was a lot of things, but she didn't remember stupid being one of them. Challenging a man like Grant Reddington was foolish at best, and downright suicide at worst. He wasn't the kind of man who lost things, a fact she knew better than anyone.

She gritted her teeth in disbelief when Griff pushed the rest of his chips into the center of the table.

Fuck shit.

She thought Griff was a good poker player at least, but it turned out he hadn't improved much since the days they'd played against each other on the basement carpet, while the old TV played reruns of I Love Lucy because they couldn't afford cable.

Leave it up to Griff to fuck up rescuing her. Not that she needed rescuing. The old Sarah might have, but Candi? Candi was in charge of her own life. Candi was paying off her debts. Candi had a plan.

At the poker table, Grant flipped the final card. Griff's girlfriend leaned forward, her watered-down drink forgotten. It was a good Cosmo, but Sarah could tell the girl didn't like it. Apparently, they were all liars.

Sarah wasn't happy with anything happening, but the girlfriend was the one piece of the puzzle she couldn't quite sort out. Griff was notoriously picking horrible women, although he was the kind of guy who ended up dating them for a few months instead of just screwing them and moving on like a normal dude.

This one seemed different somehow. She had a stunning figure and the kind of crystalline green eyes that should be featured on the cover of Vogue, but she'd wobbled on her heels in the lush carpet. Not to mention the way she'd stiffened up when Griff kissed her, as if it was the first time. Which was weird.

She swiped at the bar with the dirty cloth, trying to ignore the tremble in her hands while the two men at the table sized each other up. Her life was fine. Sure, she was probably partying too much and hadn't called home since...last Christmas?

Had it been that long?

Well, she was twenty-two! Your twenties were for fucking up and finding out. They were for sleeping around, too many roommates, and staying out until dawn to eat waffles in a shitty diner. They were for dropping out of college, ignoring student loan payment emails, and doing a little too many mushrooms.

Which is precisely what she'd been doing when Grant Redding-ton swept into her life. She'd been waitressing at a local sports bar on the weekend for extra cash and stealing from the register when it suited her. They really should have upgraded to Toast or some other digital system, but the owner insisted on keeping the cash register from the 90s and garnishing the tips "for the kitchen" (i.e., himself).

She'd been on the brink of being fired when Grant came in one agonizingly slow Sunday afternoon with his golf buddies. He was handsome and rich, and had taken her home instead of just wanti-ng to fuck behind the restaurant. He'd been so nice at first, buying her clothes from stores with appointment hours and whisking her away to his ski chalet in Aspen for the weekend.

She wasn't stupid. He'd been using her, as much as she'd been using him. She just wasn't sure when the tides had turned. It was probably when he'd helped her get out of a little bit of credit card debt. Or maybe after he'd stopped her shitty Honda Civic from getting repossessed. It was pocket money to him, but somehow, she'd morphed from arm candy to employee over the last year.

Still, she had a plan. Work off what she owed him and get the hell out. Start fresh. All she needed was a little more—

"I'll take the bartender," Griff said.

Sarah froze. The glass she'd been drying slipped from her hand, shattering on the floor. She blinked at Griff's profile, but he still didn't turn. The girlfriend looked, though, confused. Only Grant took the odd request in stride, lifting one eyebrow at her from across the room.

Shit.

"You want my...bartender?" Grant asked, amused.

Or at least he sounded amused. She could hear the rage just below the surface. If there was one thing a man like Grant Reddington hated, it was being played for a fool.

Griff's girlfriend leaned forward, hissing something in Griff's ear, but he shook it off, his eyes firmly on Grant's as he waited for a response.

Sarah swallowed. She should stop this. Should speak up for herself. Demand that they not use her as a pawn in some silly ego match, but the words pressed against the back of her teeth. The ugly truth was, she'd been waiting to be rescued—not in her head but somewhere deep, where she was too stupid to figure out how to live her own life.

The girlfriend was still staring at her, and Sarah watched the puzzle pieces fall into place in the woman's mind. Watched the shock and betrayal wash over her face. It was comforting. She wasn't the only one who'd been lied to.

"So?" Griff asked, his voice low, attention still on the game.

After a long second, Grant shrugged one shoulder and leaned back in his chair. "Seems like a bad bet to me. There are a thousand girls just like her."

Sarah winced, waiting for her brother to defend her worth, but he stayed silent. The anger in the girlfriend's eyes turned to pity, but then Grant flipped over his cards.

Even from the bar, Sarah could see the hand: two queens and two sevens, plus the one on the table. Grant had a full house. An excellent hand. A winning hand. Sarah's stomach dropped.

Griff studied Grant's hand for a second without reacting. Sarah considered crossing the room and strangling him, but then he casually leaned forward and fanned out his own cards.

"Flush," Griff said. And smiled.

Fifteen

"Are you fucking kidding me?!" Rue gasped as the BMW rocked away from Grant's mansion. She didn't bother to buckle up, turning to look at the woman in the backseat. "Your sister?"

The girl didn't answer, clinging to the door handle as Griff upshifted, taking the narrow curve in the driveway fast enough to make Rue clutch her own seat.

"Would you have helped me if I had told you the truth?" Griff responded, not taking his foot off the gas as the iron gate loomed. His voice was grim. "If this wasn't about money?"

Rue twisted forward, clambering for her seatbelt. "Of course! What kind of monster do you think I am?"

Griff grimaced and hit a button on the visor. She wasn't even surprised when the gate started to swing open.

"In my experience, strangers don't help strangers unless they have a damn good reason," he said.

Rue closed her lips around a protest as the car shot through the gate. She'd lost count of the number of people who'd come to her for help. And the number she'd turned away. People with dying parents and eviction notices pinned to their dream homes. People with broken hearts and empty wallets.

In her defense, she'd stood next to a hundred hospital beds. She had left the warmth of her home on Christmas day to find a homeless father sleeping on a bench on a subzero morning. She had watched doctors deliver healthy babies from laboring women even as the blue code light blinked above their heads.

The world was a hard, sad place, and she was just one person. It was true, but it also didn't help her sleep at night.

She said none of this as Griff turned onto the highway, tires squealing, although no one appeared to be following them.

"I'm sorry I didn't tell you about the game. About Sarah. I know it was shitty to lie..." he said, knuckles white on the wheel. "You will be compensated. I promise"

Rue didn't know how to respond. Griff wasn't great at promises, but she'd almost forgotten about the money in all the excitement. Almost.

She glanced in the backseat again as the car slowed to a normal speed. Candi (Sarah?) was still unbuckled, pressed tightly between Tug's heavy body and the door. The girl was staring at the Great Dane as if he were a mirage. Tug, unbothered by her inspection, drooled on her arm.

Sarah looked a lot less sophisticated tumbling around the back of Griff's car in her red sequin dress. Her bleached hair needed a wash, the waves barely held together by dry shampoo. The street lights outside flickered by, catching on the hollowness of her cheeks. She had the same eyes as Griff, smoky blue-gray, but there was an emptiness behind them that couldn't be hidden by makeup.

She was a bar bathroom girl. The kind who drank tequila too fast and had a phone full of unanswered texts from a shitty boyfriend. The kind with smeared mascara and puke on their collar. Rue had never been that girl—she wasn't cool enough or wild enough—but she'd always wanted to be. Wanted to dance on tables in black lace bras with her girlfriends and fly to Ibiza with nothing more than a passport.

Those girls couldn't be more different from her, with her DoorDash Fridays and couch nest and silent phones, but she felt a kinship to them. It was just a different kind of lonely.

"You okay?" Rue asked Sarah gently. Griff finally glanced in the rearview mirror at his sister. His lips were a flat line.

Sarah squinted at Tug, her head lolling on the seat as if it was too heavy to hold up. "Do you see a really, really big dog? Like horse-sized?"

Rue smiled. "That's Tugboat."

Tug cocked his head at his name and then licked the side of Sarah's face. She wrinkled her nose, but didn't bother moving.

"Sorry," Rue said. "He has mommy issues."

Sarah huffed out a laugh. "Are you his girlfriend?" she asked, nodding at the back of Griff's head.

Rue didn't look at him. There was no point in thinking about the earlier kiss or the inconvenient way it seemed to be burned into her skin. "No."

"Smart. He's an asshole."

Griff glared at his sister in the rearview mirror. "In a lineup, I'm definitely not the asshole in this situation."

It was the wrong thing to say. Sarah crossed her arms and glared out the window. Griff grimaced at the windshield and fell silent.

Rue lifted an eyebrow, reminded that having an actual family that loved you wasn't all cozy Thanksgiving dinners and holding newborn cousins like on TV. She rummaged in her purse instead of acknowledging the awkward silence, pulling out a bottle of ibuprofen. She handed it back along with a half-empty bottle of water. Sarah grunted a thank you and popped the pills.

A few beats later she poked her head between the seats, one arm around Tug's neck. Sarah squinted at the closest highway sign. "Where are you taking me?"

Griff's fingers flexed on the steering wheel. "Rehab."

Sarah flopped back with a hu "You suck."

***

Rue was surprised when Griff pulled onto her street an hour later. It was almost morning, just a hint of light visible on the horizon, early enough for every parking spot to still be taken and the blue recycling bins to be on the curb.

He double-parked alongside her car. There was a deflated blow-up snowman on the small patch of grass in front of her small apartment complex, listing to the side in the gray snow.

She *shouldn't* be surprised, of course. The job was done. The agreement they'd reached had been satisfied. Griff's prize was snoring in the backseat, half covered by Tugboat's sleeping body. She was officially being un-kidnapped, which was precisely what she wanted. So why did it feel like losing a book right before the last chapter?

The engine purred quietly, the wipers flicking away the tiniest flakes of snow that dotted the glass.

"I'm sorry about all this," Griff said, waving at Sarah in the backseat.

The words "no problem" tried to jump out of her mouth, like it wouldn't do to let her kidnapper know that his side quest had been a huge inconvenience, but that would be a people-pleasing lie.

She had a life, after all, but, for some reason, she found herself fumbling for her keys as if they weren't right inside her tote. Rue cleared her throat. "What about the...um, money?"

And the kiss, her brain whispered.

She yanked her keys out of her tote and told her brain to kindly shut the fuck up.

Griff held up his phone. "I need to liquify some assets, which will take a minute, but the funds should be in your account by next Monday."

She nodded, trying to summon up the giddiness that kind of money should invoke. It was a life-changing amount. It was enough to start over. Maybe start her own shelter somewhere and meet someone who was less into crimes and then—

Her mind stuttered. And then...what? Start a family? Get a fancy car? Try to scrounge up some real friends?

"Are you okay?" Griff asked, clearly wondering why she was still sitting in his car. His face was hidden in shadow, but she remembered the exact shape of his mouth. She thought about how he had used it back at Grant's—hard and soft at the same time. He probably was the same in bed—all teeth and feather soft touches.

Shit fuck shit.

Rue climbed out of the car and shouldered her bag. It occurred to her that she didn't have Griff's number. Or where he lived. Suddenly, the whole fiasco felt like just another failed Hinge date—a good story to tell at a party and nothing more. She swallowed the lump in her throat, reminding herself that the reason she didn't know where Griff lived was because she'd arrived in the trunk of his car.

"You don't seem happy for someone who just came into a shit ton of money," Griff observed over the car roof. He opened the door for Tug, who bounded out as if they were getting back from a walk in the park instead of a bona fide caper.

"I'm still locked out of my fucking house," she said. A lie was much easier than the mortifying truth.

"Oh, shit, sorry." Griff ran a hand through his hair, smiling ruefully. He still wasn't wearing a coat, and his shoulders were hunched in from the cold. "I forgot to mention I sent out a locksmith while you were at the cabin."

He grabbed her suitcase from the trunk, setting it on the icy sidewalk before digging in his back pocket and producing a shiny key attached to a plastic business card that said, "Ruby's Locksmith LLC," and featured a cartoon of a dancing key.

Griff dropped it into her hand without touching her. "Again, sorry about all this."

As if he had just stepped on her toe or spilled coffee on her lap instead of kidnapping her for three days.

"I don't forgive you," she teased. He was standing too close, and she could see the bits of fairy snow that clung to his eyelashes. He smelled like whiskey, the bastard.

Griff lifted one very attractive eyebrow. "No?"

Rue considered kissing him. The kind of goodbye kiss that would keep her warm during the lonely winter nights. The kind she could write about in her journal or use to convince her mom she was "fine".

The kind of kiss that seemed harmless but cut deep. Rue grabbed her suitcase and called Tug, who bounded happily toward her from the hydrant he was investigating, before stepping away. She'd had enough of those kisses to last a lifetime.

Sixteen

For the next three days, Griff tried not to think about Rue.

He distracted himself by getting Sarah reluctantly settled in her (very expensive) rehab center. She fought him every step of the way, insisting that she didn't "need his damn help," but she eventually gave in after discovering her shitty roommates had hawked all her stuff on Marketplace because she hadn't paid her share of the rent.

Then there was nothing left to do but wait and hope. He tried to keep busy shoveling the endlessly accumulating snow and brushing up on online poker, but on the fourth day, he gave up, backing his old F150 out of the garage. Turnip panted happily in the passenger seat, his hot breath fogging the window as he watched them pull onto the highway. His squashed nose left marks on the glass.

For the first time in days, Griff's shoulders relaxed. He hated doing nothing, and the stupid old truck was one of his favorite things, bought off a geezer in overalls and a stained baseball cap for 2k (cash, of course).

It was ancient, with a rust-red finish where the paint still clung. The old girl rattled on the straightaways and coughed black smoke when the hills got too steep. The plaid fabric on the bench seat was worn in enough places that Griff had thrown a wool blanket over the whole thing. It had been his first big purchase when he turned nineteen, and the money from his winnings started to roll in. He didn't have the heart to sell it.

Now he used the old truck to gather intel on his opponents. It was conveniently invisible when he had to stalk some rich asshole while they cheated on their wives in seedy motels or negotiated backward business deals in empty parking lots. Knowing the other players at the poker table was his secret weapon, and it had come in clutch more times than he could count.

Today was different, though. He suspected that Rue wouldn't be surprised to find him on her doorstep again. Maybe she'd even invite him inside.

Griff cracked the window. It was unseasonably warm for the end of January—one of those 56-degree winter days that made you forget that the cold was just starting to get comfortable. The wind ruffled his hair, and he had to reach for his sunglasses. Turnip wedged himself against Griff's hip, and he turned up the radio. The dog made a surprisingly sturdy armrest.

The day would have been perfect if he hadn't had to check in on Sarah. Griff sighed. "Siri, call Turning Point."

It had been a complicated production to install Bluetooth in the old truck, including two trips to Best Buy, but he'd finally managed. The phone rang twice through the static speakers before a hollow voice answered, "Turning Point. How may I direct your call?"

He rolled his window back up. "This is Griff Banks calling to check up on the status of a patient: Sarah Banks."

"Of course! Just a moment, please." There was a pause. Keys clattered underneath the hiss of static, and then the secretary cleared her throat.

Griff's stomach bottomed out. He listened numbly to the muffled whispers on the other side of the line as the secretary talked with someone else at the desk. He swore, glancing in the rearview mirror before pulling onto the side of the highway.

The line cleared. There was a long beat of awkward silence.

"She checked herself out?" he asked, saving the secretary from having to say it.

"I'm afraid so, sir."

The truck sputtered and stalled in the turnoff, adding insult to injury. "When? Did she leave an address? Say where she was going?"

"I'm afraid I can't give out that information. Turning Point is a self-check-in/self-check-out facility, and we pride ourselves in..."

Griff tuned out the rest of her customer service speech, staring blankly out the windshield. The truck shuddered as a Semi flew by. He knew the deal. He'd been through this a half dozen times before, but for some reason, it hurt more today. This time, Sarah may have cost him more than he had to give.

He thanked the woman and hung up, pulling his phone out from under Turnip's snoring body. Sarah wasn't dumb, but she probably had other things on her mind, which meant she probably hadn't found the AirTag he'd hidden in her backpack before leaving her at Turning Point. He hit the Find My Phone app, holding his breath until her circle blipped to life on the map.

Griff blinked, immediately recognizing the address. Because he'd been heading there himself.

Motherfucker.

***

Rue studied the girl curled against her apartment door.

Sarah was asleep, her head resting at an odd angle underneath the doorknob. Her hair was shorter than the last time Rue'd seen her, cut into a surprisingly chic bob that ended abruptly at her chin.

The girl was shivering despite the long puffer coat tucked around her knees like a sleeping bag. The apartment's overhang kept the weather from her face, but a light dusting of snow had accumulated on her lower half. Tug sniffed her sneakers politely. Sarah shifted but didn't wake.

Rue sighed. This was the last thing she needed on a Tuesday in the middle of winter. After a long adoption event at work, all she wanted to do was take a hot shower, eat two bowls of Frosted Flakes, and sleep until summer. Instead, she'd be babysitting Griff's kid sister.

Unfortunately, the jerk hadn't left his number, or she would have been calling him to—

"Oh! You're here," Sarah said, her voice still groggy. She staggered to a standing position, using the door for leverage, a little unsteady as she brushed the snow from her coat. For a second, Rue thought she might be high, but there was brightness to her blue eyes as she patted Tug's head that suggested otherwise.

"I guess you're wondering what I'm doing here," Sarah said. Her smile was annoyingly hopeful.

Rue humphed and jingled her keys. Sarah jumped to the side, biting her lip as Rue brushed past her to unlock the front door.

"Shouldn't you be at Turning Point?" Rue asked, pushing inside and tossing her work tote onto the couch. The apartment still smelled vaguely like an old washcloth. She paused to light one of the candles David had left behind.

"I was!" Sarah said from the open doorway. "I did. It was only a short program. But then—"

"Come inside." Rue interrupted. "My landlord keeps the thermostat at 65 in the winter, the bastard."

Sarah hesitated before taking one step into the apartment and closing the door behind her, as if it hadn't been her idea to stop by unannounced in the first place.

"Are you going to call Griff on me?" she asked.

Rue shrugged off her coat as the girl shifted nervously on the welcome mat.

Griff had told her a little about Sarah while his sister slept off her hangover in the backseat, but it had been the big brother version. He'd told her about a little girl who loved swimming and had an unhealthy obsession with stuffed dolphins and K-pop. He had told her about Sarah's first year of art school, how she started missing classes in the second semester, and how she hadn't come home from spring break. He'd told her about the four desperate years that followed.

Rue didn't see any of that precious, loved little girl. She saw a typical 23-year-old—someone who had taken a wrong turn somewhere and had lost herself.

There was a five-year age gap between them, but it felt like a gulf. Rue had never done anything reckless in her life, but there was still something about Sarah that she recognized. A version of herself she could have been if she had swerved left instead of right. If she'd met the wrong friends instead of having none at all.

If there was anything she'd learned from working at the shelter, it was that your worth didn't have anything to do with the life the world handed you.

"I don't have his number," Rue told the girl, as if that was the whole story. She turned and headed into the kitchen as Sarah inched into the apartment.

Not sure what else to do, she filled the electric kettle. She hated tea, but it seemed like the right thing to do considering the situation. She dug around in the pantry and found some Sleepy Time and a single peppermint teabag. Rue held up both, and Sarah pointed at the mint one, perched on the kitchen island stool, one foot still on the floor as if she might bolt at any time. She still hadn't taken off her coat.

"Most people would rat me out," Sarah said, blowing on her fingers, still red from her nap in the cold. The kettle started to boil.

"Everyone should be allowed to make their own mistakes. Even sisters."

Sarah's eyebrows twitched in surprise. Rue got the feeling the girl wasn't used to being forgiven.

She got two mismatched cups from the cupboard (one shaped like a jack-o-lantern and the other with just a plain mug with Becky's diner fading on the side). Maybe tea wouldn't be so bad.

Sarah watched as she poured the steaming water into the mugs. "You think I'm making a mistake? Not being in rehab?"

"Depends," Rue said, sliding Sarah's tea across the counter. "Why are you here?"

Sarah wrapped her fingers around the jack-o'-lantern and sighed. "Griff told me about your weird...talent?"

Ah. This was about Luck.

Rue took a sip of her own tea, wrinkled her nose, and reached for the sugar. She added two big scoops, but it didn't help. The tea just tasted like sweet dirt water now.

"So you want money?" she asked, trying to psych herself up for a trip to the closest gas station that sold lotto tickets.

It was late and cold and her feet hurt. The sad peanut butter sandwich she'd eaten for lunch felt like a million years ago, but Sarah laughed at the suggestion. It was a brittle sound. "I'm not as stupid as I look. If I had money, I'd just blow it on drugs and booze and end up right back where I started."

Rue's brow furrowed. "So?"

Sarah twisted the mug in her hands before blurting, "Can I stay with you? Just for a little while? I won't be in the way, I swear. I'll do chores—wash the dishes, watch the dog. I can't pay you...I don't have any money...but you won't even know I'm here! I swear!"

Rue blinked at the girl. Fuckity fuck.

"Don't you think Griff's house is a better place for you right now?" Rue asked carefully. "I don't know anything about...what to do with you."

Sarah's hands trembled slightly as she tried to tuck her hair behind her ear and then realized it was too short. Her eyes filled with tears. "I've done these programs before. A dozen times! And it's...not enough. I need more. A break. A little luck? I don't know. Something!"

She sobbed the last part, covering her face with her hands. Rue slumped against the counter, giving up on the tea. What she wouldn't give for a slice of pizza and a soft pillow right now.

Behind Sarah, Tug had fallen asleep on the couch, his enormous body stretched from one end to the other, his toe beans hanging off the edge. Sure, David's bedroom was empty, but he'd taken all the furniture, including the bed. She didn't even have an air mattress. There was hardly enough room for her, let alone—

BANG!

Bang bang **BANG!**

Sarah leaped off her stool, hot tea spilling over her hand. She didn't seem to notice.

They both stared at the front door. Rue had a pretty good idea who was pounding on her door, but she slipped her hand into the knife drawer anyway. A girl couldn't be too careful.

"Rue?" Griff shouted, probably waking up the whole damn complex. "Is Sarah in there with you?"

Rue sighed and let go of the cleaver. Griff didn't bother knocking again, bursting through the door with half the snow in the city on his boots and Turnip under one arm. The bulldog was wearing a bright red sweater.

Rue rubbed her forehead. She really needed to get better at locking her front door. Griff's hair stood up like a haystack, no doubt displaced by the wet beanie clutched in his hand. The collar of his coat was turned inside out, and his eyes were wild.

Meanwhile, Sarah had wedged herself in the narrow space between the kitchen island and the couch as if she was trying to blend in with the furniture. The siblings glared at each other across the apartment.

"Are you trying to wake up the whole damn complex?" Rue asked Griff mildly.

Griff kicked the door closed behind him in response. The doorjamb shuddered, and he turned his glare on her. She tried not to notice how damn cute he looked with wet hair falling in his eyes and red cheeks.

"Why do you have my sister?" he snapped, as if Rue had invited Sarah over for a cozy girl's night instead of finding her on her stoop like a damn Amazon package.

She lifted an eyebrow. "Are you serious? I thought kidnapping was cool with you?"

He huffed at that, but his shoulders relaxed an inch.

Rue wanted to be mad. She *should* be, considering the Banks family kept involving her in their family drama, but she could see Griff's thinly veiled terror behind the twitch in his jaw.

No one had ever worried about her that much. No one in her life would brave snowy roads to yell at her in the middle of the night. No one who would panic if she went missing. Not unless her Luck was involved, of course.

Sarah didn't feel the same. Her chin lifted, misery giving way to defiance at the sight of her angry older brother.

Rue stepped between them before the yelling could start, holding out a hand to Griff. "Your coat, sir."

"My coat?"

"Yes. I will take your coat and make you some Sleepy Time tea. Or... I think I have some shitty wine around here somewhere. And then we will sit down and talk about this like grown-ups."

There was some scowling and a brief argument about "hauling Sarah's ungrateful ass back to the house," but eventually both siblings caved after Rue promised to DoorDash pizza.

When it came, she kicked Tug off the couch and sat on the floor next to the coffee table, sharing slices of pepperoni with Turnip as Griff and Sarah talked and yelled and then talked some more. Eventually, two things were decided.

#1: Rue would stay at Griff's cabin for a week to help Sarah "get back on her feet," and in payment, he would add another half million to her fee.

#2 Sarah would submit to rehab if the experiment didn't work and take it "seriously this time."

Rue wasn't sure which was more unlikely.

She didn't tell them she would have done it for free. Maybe because she wasn't ready to admit it to herself.

Seventeen

Griff stared up at the ceiling fan, listening to Rue's whispers and the tippy-tap of Tug's toenails as they tried to sneak past his bedroom door. It was six in the morning.

He should have been dead asleep, considering the fiasco the night before. Turnip certainly was, his heavy body wedged awkwardly under Griff's armpit. By the time he'd negotiated with Sarah, driven them all back to the cabin, and gotten Rue situated in the guest room, it had been well after 3 am, but he'd snapped awake the second he'd heard the guest bedroom door snick open.

A muffled bang and hushed curse came from down the hall, which was immediately followed by Tug's low woof. Griff laughed quietly in the dark.

He'd been glad to see Rue last night, despite the circumstances. He couldn't stop thinking about the way her green eyes had glimmered with amusement when he burst into her apartment, or the relief he'd felt when she agreed to help them. Again.

He was trying to remember that Rue wasn't doing them a favor out of the kindness of her heart, regardless of any feelings he might have. He was paying her. This wasn't some weird extended Tinder date. Yes, they'd kissed. And sure, he'd liked it more than any kiss in recent memory, but anyone would be a fool not to enjoy kissing Rue Adler. She had sweet, kissable lips and—

There was another thump, followed by the sound of the French doors in the living room sliding open. Turnip finally lifted his head, a temporary relief to the loud, wet snores he'd been administering directly into Griff's ear all night.

"It's okay, boy," Griff whispered, rubbing the dog's soft head. Turnip snorted in response and squirmed onto his belly. The shelter said he was eight years old, which was ancient in bulldog years, but he could hold his bladder past sunrise, which meant Griff didn't have to get up for a couple more hours.

But for some reason, he found himself rising anyway. Rue was a guest. He should make sure she was comfortable, right? Should see if she needed coffee or an extra blanket. Or a spot underneath him in his bed.

Griff muttered to himself and threw on a hoodie before padding into the living room. The fire in the hearth was just ash, and the room was dark except for the light above the stove. The only sign that anyone was awake was the open sliding glass door.

He moved closer and then froze.

Rue stood alone on the snowy deck, gazing at the waning moon as it sank toward the horizon. It was startlingly bright, its perfect twin shimmering on the surface of the black ocean.

But Griff wasn't looking at the moon.

Rue was wearing one of his dress shirts as a nightgown, her arms wrapped tight around her middle to ward off the cold, her feet shoved into the too-big fur-lined boots he kept by the door. He recognized the shirt, crisp white and so outrageously expensive he kept it in the guest closet for special occasions.

She might as well have been naked.

The fabric was sheer in the moonlight, her silhouette outlined from one peaked nipple to the curve of her soft hip. A tattoo of delicate vines and flowers curled from the base of her spine before disappearing beneath the cascade of dark hair spilling down her back.

Griff had dated plenty of women. He had been with vapid runway models, painfully thin nepo babies, and snooty daughters of old money who'd had plastic surgery before they were even out of their teens—but the sight of Rue in the moonlight took his breath away.

He wanted to put his hands on her. Wanted to crush the fabric that caught and gathered on the curve of her ass in his fist and drag her against him. Wanted to see if the silver light on her skin rubbed off on his fingertips.

He took a step back, attempting to fade into the shadows, but then she turned, jumping at the sight of him standing in the dark living room like a creeper.

"Oh!" One hand went to the hollow of her throat. "Shit. I hope I didn't wake you up. I was just taking Tug out to pee—he has a very strict bathroom schedule."

Rue smiled, unaware of the heat blazing through him. She clearly had no idea how sheer her makeshift nightgown was against the moonlight. Now that she'd turned, he could clearly see the dimple of her belly button, not to mention the second tattoo, a small heart, on the inside of her thigh. Thank god, she was wearing underwear.

He should tell her. That's what a gentleman would do.

Instead, Griff cleared his throat and said, "You look cold."

"Freezing!" she said, stamping her feet and giving a playful shudder before turning to whisper-yell for Tug over the railing.

Unstuck from her gaze, Griff glanced once at the curve of her ass before ducking back into the house to grab the wool blanket from the back of the couch.

Rue gestured up at the moon when he stepped back onto the deck. "Did you see?"

The moon glowed like a gem above the dark water. Griff didn't take his eyes from her face. "Beautiful."

For the first time, Rue seemed to notice something unusual about their conversation. Her smile hitched.

He held up the blanket and moved closer. "May I?"

She nodded, her teeth worrying her bottom lip. Griff tried desperately not to think about the way those lips would look around his...

He wrapped the blanket around her shoulders, but couldn't seem to make himself step back once she was covered, so he pretended to straighten the fabric. Her hair smelled like the sea and girly shampoo. Maybe he wasn't a gentleman at all.

"Thank you," Rue said, smiling up at him and clutching the blanket against her throat.

He nodded, mouth dry. Her body had disappeared under the blanket, and somehow it was even worse because he could imagine himself peeling it back like a god damn Christmas gift.

"Griff?" she breathed.

His hand was still on her shoulder, thumb touching the soft skin of her neck as if by accident. It wasn't.

Rue was blushing, as if she could read his thoughts, the pale pink tint blooming on her cheeks, and suddenly, he didn't care if he was paying her or kidnapping her or dating her. He just wanted to see if her lips were warm.

Griff leaned forward to find out.

It was barely a kiss, just a brush of soft skin at first, but then she sighed, and he couldn't help but sink into her.

Cold. Her lips were cold, he thought idly. His hand cupped her jaw as she moved closer, one of her bare legs slipping between his own. He was already hard. Her thigh pressed lightly against him there, and she gasped softly, although it couldn't have been a surprise.

Suddenly, he was yanking her closer, fingertips pressing divots into her skin. It was rough. Too rough. But she was with him, hands pressed hard between his shoulder blades as if she could absorb him. The blanket was a puddle around their feet, and his hands were sliding over her hips, lifting her.

She made a sound in the back of her throat, and he must have blacked out because the next minute she was pressed against the side of the house, and he was devouring her neck, her pulse fluttering against his lips. Griff thought Rue would be the kind of girl who liked feather touches and flirting, but her hands dipped below the waistband of his pajamas, clever fingers wrapping around his length. It was his turn to make a sound.

It would have taken nothing to slip inside her. To strip them both and dive into that heat. Push her against the wall, even outside, here in the dark on his back deck with the cold—

Something nudged his hip.

And woofed.

Griff ripped his mouth from Rue's, resting his head on her shoulder as Tug danced around them in the snow.

"Tug, I will kill you," Rue whimpered, her head thrown back, lips wet and swollen. She looked like a god damn wet dream. He wanted...wanted...

Tug barked. Louder this time.

Beside Rue's head, the kitchen light flicked on inside the house. Griff swore. He had her pressed right beside the window, tucked into the shadows, but the kitchen light glowed cheerfully onto the blanket Rue had left behind in the snow.

"Shit," Rue whispered, as he set her reluctantly back on the deck to the familiar sound of the coffee pot bubbling to life on the other side of the wall. The dishwasher opened. Cups clicked quietly on the counter.

The French doors were still open a crack, and cold air was seeping into the living room. It was only a matter of moments before his damn sister would come out here to see why.

Now that they weren't devouring each other, he could feel the goosebumps on Rue's arms and see the heat of his own breath. He almost fucked her outside in the middle of the damn winter. She should be laid out on his king-sized bed, naked and warm. Still, he couldn't bring himself to pull away, and she seemed to be having similar problems. Her fingers were still tangled in his hair, her chest heaving.

"We're adults," she breathed into his neck. He couldn't tell by her tone if there was regret in her voice. He hoped not because he intended to finish what they'd started.

"I'll go around to the front door," he answered, tasting her lips one last time before finally letting go. "She won't suspect anything."

Ruth laughed softly. The sound trickled down his spine. "Good plan."

***

"So now what?" Sarah asked.

Rue shoveled the last bite of pancake into her mouth and tried not to look at Griff's little sister, who was sitting cross-legged on the kitchen counter with her own heaping plate of flapjacks.

Sarah looked terrible. Her sleep shirt was comically oversized and hung limply from one shoulder. There were deep bruises underneath her bloodshot eyes, but she was on her third serving of pancakes, so that must mean something.

Sarah hadn't bought any of their "oops, I was just outside walking the dog" routine and had teased Griff all morning, until he snapped at her with a damp kitchen towel and referenced a toxic high school boyfriend. She'd clammed up after that.

Rue wasn't used to sibling banter, but she'd relaxed after Griff threw her a playful wink while flipping bacon. Now, he was leaning against the sink, looking sinful in his bare feet and mussed morning hair. He sipped his third cup of coffee and avoided her eyes.

"Now what, what?" Griff asked his sister.

Sarah waved a fork. Syrup splattered on Griff's pristine cabinets. "We can't just sit around staring at each other all week."

"No?"

"Griff Banks, my life is depressing enough as it is! Let's DO something."

"This isn't a vacation."

He turned to put his mug in the sink. Sarah set down her plate. Her hand shook lightly, but her tone was light. "What, Mr. Moneybags can't afford a little fun?"

Griff rolled his eyes and started washing dishes while Sarah pouted at the back of his head.

"I think a little fun might be nice," Rue interjected quietly.

Sarah brightened. "Ooh, how about rock climbing? Or white water rafting? I saw a sign back at the bottom of the mountain for it!"

Rue's eyes widened. She considered herself indoorsy at best. She preferred to keep her feet firmly on the ground.

"Sarah, it's January," Griff said over his shoulder, in a tone that implied that he was very used to Sarah's harebrained ideas.

"What about an '80s movie night?" Rue suggested, tentatively. "Maybe I could make dinner?"

"Yessss," Sarah hissed, clapping her hands. She jumped down from the counter and headed to her bedroom, calling, "We leave in 20!"

Griff turned, hands dripping soap. "What? Where?"

"The grocery store! And that little retro DVD place in town," Sarah yelled from the other room.

"We can stream any movie in the world..." he trailed off when Sarah's bedroom door slammed. Griff shook his head, glowering over at her. "Traitor."

"You had other big plans?" she teased.

His eyes darkened in response, and Rue flushed, realizing what plans he was imagining.

She stood abruptly, the stool screeching behind her. "I'll...get the groceries," she stammered, backing toward the guest room. "I'm a pretty good cook. Actually. Um, maybe some steak? Do you eat steak? Of course, you do."

Griff's expression had morphed from hungry wolf to amusement.

"You don't have to do that," he said, drying his hands on a towel. "Cook for us, I mean."

"I want to!" she responded and fled.

Eighteen

Sarah didn't look at the duffel bag she'd tossed in the corner of Griff's guest room, dressing quickly in one of the three outfits she still had after her shitty roommates sold all her stuff. She knew from experience that it was best to keep moving when things were bad. Moving meant less thinking, and thinking was the first door to depression.

She couldn't afford to wallow under the covers in her own filth for months. Not this time. Not again.

She stepped into the bathroom attached to one of Griff's many guest rooms, annoyed by the gleaming chrome and the rainfall shower head. It was nice, not in a Grant Reddington mansion kind of way, but a million miles from the rundown bathrooms in her last rental with its black molding and dripping faucet.

Her hands trembled as she sprayed her roots with dry shampoo and then ran a brush through her hair, wincing at the tangles. The ends were brittle from too much box bleach, but she hated the idea of cutting her hair even shorter than she already had. It felt like defeat, as if the drugs had succeeded in taking a part of her.

They hadn't, Sarah told herself firmly, avoiding her eyes in the mirror while she brushed her teeth. The pills stashed in the bottom of her duffel bag were just a bit of insurance. No one understood how hard it was to quit after a few years of partying, not rehab, and definitely not Griff, the self-righteous asshole. She might need a little something to steady herself. Wasn't 95% sober good enough?

No, her mind whispered. All or nothing was the only way in this fucked up world. Black or white. Win or lose. And she had never won.

Sarah finally looked at her reflection. The girl staring back at her lacked her usual fun sparkle. She was too thin and paler than any self-tanner could fix, but it wasn't her physical appearance that gave away how lost she was. There was a flatness to her face as if she'd been run through a gray filter on Instagram. It was a miracle anyone had wanted to fuck her, let alone Grant Reddington.

She would have chalked it up to a pity lay if he wasn't such an asshole. It was a mystery that should have bothered her more, but as the months went on at the mansion, she'd cared less and less about—

"You ready?" Griff called from the hallway.

Sarah turned, grateful to leave her reflection behind, and stepped back into the guest bedroom. Griff stood awkwardly in the doorway, looking like he'd just stepped out of a J Crew camping advertisement, from his scuffed Blundstones to the wool sailors' beanie. It was annoying as hell.

"Rue's already in the car," he said, hands shoved into his coat.

"You let her sit up front this time? Or is she in the trunk?" she asked, shrugging on the puffer jacket she bought at Goodwill for 6$.

"You're bringing up my bad choices a lot for someone who skipped out of her 20k dollar halfway house program."

Sarah's stomach hollowed. "I didn't ask you to do that."

She didn't look at the duffel bag in the corner, deciding at that exact moment that she didn't need an insurance plan. She was tired of being a fuck up, but she sure as hell wasn't going to give Griff the satisfaction of being the one to save her. He'd never let her forget it.

She'd flush those pills when they got back. Sarah wasn't sure if all the luck mumbo jumbo about Rue was real, but at this point, she was willing to try anything.

"You're welcome," Griff snapped when she didn't answer, and then swallowed as if holding back more words.

Asshole.

She gave him a fake bow and then pushed past him into the hallway. He stank of expensive cologne. Her head pounded, and the extra pancake was sitting like a ball of lead in her stomach. Being fully awake and conscious was hellish enough without being lectured.

Griff followed her, staying blissfully silent while they piled into the car. Sarah sat in the back with the dogs, which she would have been annoyed about if they weren't so damn cute and soft. Turnip lay in her lap like a lump while Tug stood over them both to look out the window.

Griff chatted with Rue as they drove into town, talking about football and recipes and other mundane things as if this wasn't the weirdest situation on the planet. It wasn't until they dropped Rue at the little market that Sarah realized she'd foolishly set herself up to spend the morning talking to her brother.

She cleared her throat. "So. Rue, huh?"

Griff slid her a warning glance as they pulled into the video store parking lot . He didn't like to talk about himself, but she was desperate to avoid any analysis of her own fuck ups. Especially the recent ones.

"What about her?"

"You hitting that?" It was immature, but she couldn't pass up an opportunity to rile him. She had so few pleasures left in life.

He glared at her before getting out of the car. "That's none of your business."

Sarah followed him into the store, ignoring his attempt to hold the door for her. Convenient how his life was none of her business, while hers was front page news in his, but she decided to let it go. The throbbing pain in her head had erupted into sharp stabs behind her left eye, and she didn't have it in her to argue, even with Griff.

The dim store was small but surprisingly busy for such a small town, with rows of old DVDs facing out on shelves like they had in 90s Blockbuster stores. A bundled-up couple discussed the merits of action vs romcom a little too loudly in the closest aisle.

A teenager with acne and an AC/DC shirt scrolled through his phone behind the register.

They drifted toward a section labeled "Cult Classics."

"How about this?" Griff held up a battered copy of "Gremlins".

"Do you know if Rue does scary?" she asked.

Griff frowned down at the movie, a complicated set of emotions flickering across his face. He clearly had no idea what kind of movies Rue preferred, a reminder that this little fake family they were pretending to be wasn't remotely real.

"You like this girl, huh?" Sarah asked, examining the shelves.

Griff shrugged, and they debated the merits of various movies before settling on Ghostbusters, When Harry Met Sally, and Die Hard. It wasn't until they'd checked out and started driving back toward the market that Griff broke the silence.

"Do you think she can help you? Us?" he asked, tapping one finger on the steering wheel nervously. "With the Luck, I mean."

Sarah had to tuck her hands underneath her thighs to keep them from trembling, but there was no ignoring the yawning hollowness behind her sternum. It seemed bigger than the capacity of her chest to hold, a black void of ignored sadness that she usually silenced with partying and bad choices.

She pressed her head against the cold window, watching the dappled sun play across the gray snow that had collected on the edges of the road as they passed. "I hope so."

And for the first time in a long time, she meant it.

***

She decided on braised short ribs over goat cheese mashed potatoes and a side salad.

Rue was pleasantly surprised by the selection of meat and produce at the tiny market. It was a specialty shop that catered to the rich living on the outskirts of Portland. There was a pretty cheesemonger with rosy cheeks in the back who helped her pick out her cheese, and a gruff man wearing a stained apron who wrapped her meat in butcher paper. There was a decent selection of wine, which she reluctantly passed up for Sarah's sake, loading the cart with an absurd variety of fancy sodas instead.

Quiet music played overhead as she picked out a sprigs of rosemary and thyme. She stopped to smile at a toddler blowing spit bubbles in her mom's shopping cart before going in search of beef broth.

She loved to cook. It wasn't something she'd learned from her mom, who'd spent her childhood bouncing between the keto diet and green juices as long as she could remember. Their pantry had always been filled with sugar-free cookies and bran cereal. On the rare occasion her mom did cook, it was always bland, featuring salmon seasoned with (salt-free) lemon pepper or naked chicken breast over tasteless brown rice.

She'd taught herself a few years ago, devouring cookbooks checked out from the library and watching every season of The British Baking Show. It was a good hobby. One of the few that actually stuck with her. Making menus and chopping vegetables occupied the long, lonely nights, and the smell of cooking filled the space where family should have been.

Rue hummed quietly as she inspected her cart and then decided to add a batch of cookies to her plan. What was a movie night without a little treat?

She wandered back towards the baking aisle. There was no hurry. When Griff and Sarah dropped her off, they'd been arguing the merits of Ferris Bueller vs Pretty in Pink. She suspected she had plenty of time. Rue added flour and chocolate chips to her cart before considering the spices. Nutmeg or Cinnamon?

The song on the radio had switched to something upbeat, and the scarf she'd borrowed from the hall closet smelled like Griff—smoke and bergamot cologne. She wasn't sure what the next few weeks would hold, but she could still feel how soft his lips—

She was happy. Rue blinked. She almost hadn't recognized the warm feeling in her chest, but it was definitely happiness.

The last time she'd made a fancy meal had been New Year's Eve. It had been a 4-oz filet mignon and a single baked potato paired with an 8$ bottle of wine from Trader Joe's. She'd played a Spotify playlist full of old jazz classics while she cooked, bought herself a new vacuum on Amazon, and fallen asleep scrolling Tik Tok before the ball even dropped. It had been terrible.

Sarah and Griff were strangers, but at least, for right now, they were hers. Their banter made her chest ache. It had the comforting flow of old inside jokes and love, something she'd never really known.

"Excuse me."

Rue jumped, startled by the stranger waiting patiently for her to get out of the middle of the aisle.

"Oh! Sorry." Blushing, she moved aside, still clutching her nutmeg. The woman waved a forgiving hand. She was wrapped in an enormous black fur coat that reminded Rue of her mother, her face half hidden by a gray scarf. A matching hat was pulled down so far only her eyes were visible.

"Crying in the grocery store, huh?" the woman asked sympathetically, reaching past her for the smoked paprika. She had a mild accent that Rue couldn't place. Two bottles of wine and a loaf of sourdough were the only things in her cart.

"Yeah, it happens," Rue answered, mortified.

"Well, the liquor store is two doors down if you need it," the woman said, giving her a wink. Rue laughed politely as the stranger disappeared around the corner. She was being ridiculous, crying in some random grocery store like Cameron Diaz in The Holiday.

Her phone buzzed inside her coat pocket, but she didn't bother checking it, tossing the nutmeg in the cart. Griff and Sarah were waiting for her outside. She headed for the checkout line, wiping away tears.

Nineteen

I t was hard to clean out a fireplace and gawk at a beautiful woman simultaneously, but Griff was doing his best. There was something hypnotic about how Rue moved through the kitchen, going from searing meat to chopping onions with comfortable grace. She hummed as she stirred a bubbling pot, pushing back strands of hair that had escaped from her loose bun with her forearm.

"Pissst," Sarah hissed, waving a tin bucket of ashes. There was a gray smudge on her cheek. She rolled her eyes in Rue's direction and pretended to gag.

"Grow up," Griff whispered, taking the bucket and handing her a bundle of kindling. His hands were sticky with sap, but there was a new stack of firewood against the wall. He was sweating underneath his coat.

They finished setting up the fire (which Sarah had insisted was necessary for movie night) while the room filled with the smells of herbs and wine. The dogs were sleeping in a puddle on the couch. The forecast for the evening called for freezing rain.

After Griff lit the fire, Sarah stood back to admire their work. Her cheeks were rosy, and there were pine needles in her hair. She looked happier than he'd seen her in years. His heart squeezed. He knew better than to hope when it came to his sister, but he couldn't help himself. Something felt different this time.

In the kitchen, the "different" added a glug of beef broth to a Dutch oven.

Sarah nudged him in the side. "You could at least try to be subtle. You're practically eye fucking her from—"

"Shut your face," he interrupted, drawing an imaginary knife across his throat and glancing over at Rue.

Thankfully, she was absorbed in cooking. Not that it mattered. He had made it pretty clear how he felt this morning, and if she was still unsure, he intended to clarify as soon as possible.

It wasn't until a few hours later that his evening plans began to twist into doubt. Rue hadn't so much as accidentally brushed his hand or sent him a flirty wink all day, not even when they'd piled onto the couch together to watch the movie.

Her friendliness made his blood heat. He wanted to pull her underneath him until the polite burned away.

Now, she sat in his favorite leather armchair, her legs tucked underneath a wool blanket and sipping a glass of Prosecco, which she'd only agreed to after Sarah said it was okay. Her hair had finally won the battle with the ponytail holder, and it fell in a soft mess around her shoulders. Every bit of her looked soft.

It made his fingertips itch.

She smiled at him when he handed her a bowl of steaming short ribs, before reluctantly returning to couch with his own meal.

"This is fucking delicious," Sarah announced. She was curled on the other end of the couch with Tug sprawled between them. "Are you magical?"

Rue shrugged, tasting her own magic. "It's just a good recipe."

"Yeah, no," Sarah said, soaking up the rich sauce with a hunk of bread. "We're not used to good food around here unless it comes from a restaurant. Griff once tried to make a pot roast in the crockpot, and it came out somehow too dry and too wet? I don't know how that's even possible."

Griff threw a piece of bread at her, which bounced off her head and directly into Tug's open mouth. The dog licked his lips, but didn't get up, looking over his shoulder expectantly at Griff.

"Seriously," he said, addressing Rue and ignoring her ridiculous dog. "This is approximately a thousand times better than the last dinner we had. I DoorDashed General Tso's and ate alone in the dark."

They were silly, throwaway words, but Sarah's smile faded, and Rue fell silent. After a few moments of awkward fork clinking, Griff tossed another hunk of bread at Sarah's head, and this time, she caught it.

"I'm glad you're here, kid."

Griff wasn't sure why he hadn't said it until then. Sarah fiddled with her fork and didn't respond.

"So, Sarah, what do you want to do now that you're...better?" Rue asked, smoothly interrupting the silence again. "Or is that a loaded question? I always hate when people ask me what I want to do with my life."

"I was thinking about going back to school," Sarah responded. "I always wanted to be a marine biologist. Maybe community college."

"Oh, cool," Rue said, setting her empty bowl on the side table and stretching out her legs as if Sarah hadn't just said the most outrageous thing Griff had ever heard. "I took an ecobiology class in college as an elective. The labs were hard, but it was actually pretty interesting."

Griff held still as the conversation continued on to student loans and high school equivalency tests, as if Sarah's future were a given. As if she hadn't been a ghost for the past seven years. It was the first time he'd ever heard her want anything but chaos.

"So what's it like being Lucky?" Sarah asked, scratching Tug's chin. Griff snapped back to the conversation.

Rue stared into the crackling fire while Turnip crawled into her lap. "It's fine. I'm just a rabbit's foot, you know? A horseshoe above a door. A four-leaf clover. A novelty. It's exciting for a while and then..." She shrugged, thumping the dog's belly affectionately. "I guess, the excitement fades."

Sarah scrunched her nose, taking a sip of her soda. "So you get to watch everyone get their wildest dreams, and you're what? Just stuck working, paying taxes, and being boringly normal?"

Rue laughed, but it didn't reach her eyes. "That pretty much sums it up."

"Well, that sucks."

"You're telling me."

Sarah leaned forward, ignoring Griff's silent "shut up and leave her alone" look. "Tell us something that happened to you that wouldn't happen to other people. You must have good stories at least!"

Rue tilted her head, thinking. "Hmm, well, I've had three boyfriends find their soul mates while I was dating them—none of whom was me."

Sarah's eyes widened. "Oh shit."

"Yeah, it's an unfortunate side effect."

Griff's chest tightened at the idea of Rue having one boyfriend, let alone three, but she went on. "When I was eight, our neighbor figured out I was good luck because he kept getting promoted at work even though he was shit at his job. He alerted the local media. I became a town hero, which was cool for approximately three weeks, until people began to camp out on our lawn."

"What did you do?" Griff asked, watching the firelight dance in her eyes.

Rue bit her lip, remembering. "Moved. We moved a lot when I was little—rural towns, big cities, isolated cabins—my mom tried everything to keep me for herself."

Griff frowned. It was a weird way to put things. It seemed like any good parents would move around to protect their kid in this situation.

"So it's not as fun as it sounds?" Sarah asked.

Rue played with the blanket's fringe. Her eyes never left the fire. "Not even a little."

***

Rue stayed in the chair while the siblings cleaned the dishes, catching up on emails and scrolling socials. She was too cozy to help, and the warm fire threatened to lull her to sleep. After a dish of ice cream each, Sarah headed off to bed with a wave, the dogs trotting happily behind her in search of a more snuggly spot than the couch.

Griff moved quietly through the room, turning out some lights and dimming others. He stopped to throw more wood on the fire before refilling her wine and returning to his end of the couch. Rue smothered her disappointment. She'd expected him to hold out a hand and lead her to the bedroom as soon as Sarah's bedroom door closed.

Maybe she'd read the signals wrong? She didn't think so. Griff hadn't been subtle with the direction of his gaze (or thoughts) all day. Her skin felt singed underneath her sweater as if each stray glance had burned.

She was usually good at hiding her emotions. She had spent a lifetime being a blank slate for people to write on, but today had been a challenge. Underneath her calm exterior, she was jittery with anticipation.

"So," she said, trying to break the silence. "Sarah seems—"

"I don't want to talk about Sarah," Griff interrupted gently.

He'd put his pajamas on after dinner, and his hair was ruffled. He looked soft and comfortable. The sort of man you snuggled up with on the couch on a rainy day. But the heat in his eyes was unmistakable.

She tried to take a breath, but it caught in her chest. "What *do* you want to talk about?"

"I don't want to talk, Rue."

She blushed, the heat clawing up her cheeks. There was other heat, too, deep and low. "Oh."

The firelight flickered over the angles of his face, but he didn't move, his eyes dark and serious.

"If you want....you can..." She waved a hand between them awkwardly.

He shook his head, settling one hand on the arm of the couch. "What do *you* want?"

She blinked at him, confused. "Want?"

He licked his lips as if already tasting her.

Rue's eyes snared on his mouth, watching as it formed the next words. "I've been a selfish asshole since the minute we met. You've been so kind and generous...I'm not taking anything more from you. I think you've had enough of that in your life."

Rue laughed nervously. The asshole part was undoubtedly true, but sex was different than Luck. She *wanted* to be with him, as if it wasn't obvious from the way she'd nearly jumped him this morning. But she wasn't good at the wooing part. She'd always been the woo-ie.

"I...you wouldn't be!" she insisted, fidgeting with the fringe of her blanket. "Taking anything from me. I want you to, uh, you know."

"Come take what you want, then," he said quietly.

Oh.

Rue blushed so hard it burned all the way down to her sternum. She put a hand on her cheek, grateful the room was dark enough to hide the color, but there was nowhere to escape the intensity of Griff's gaze.

Her mind wanted to get ahead of any humiliation by shrugging off the moment. Maybe say something silly to break the tension. She'd been left behind so many times, and it would be stupid to be vulnerable.

Griff was waiting patiently for her decision, shoulders relaxed, and quiet knowing just below the stark desire on his face. He couldn't seem to see her fear, so Rue decided not to see it either.

His jaw twitched when she uncurled from the chair, letting the blanket pool on the floor behind her. She was wearing his white button-down from the morning and a silly pair of pink pajama shorts decorated with yellow smiley faces. It wasn't a sexy outfit, but you wouldn't know it from the way Griff's hand clenched.

Heart in her throat, Rue stepped around the coffee table, the heat of the fireplace on her back. The rug was soft underneath her bare feet. She licked her lips, nervously. Griff's eyes never left her face.

She'd have to fix that.

Rue reached behind her and pulled the shirt over her head in one motion, shaking out her hair. She wasn't wearing anything underneath. Griff's pupils dilated, and he made a sound that was suspiciously like a growl.

She'd always been shy about her body. Her stomach was soft, and there was a crease across her belly button where it rolled and dipped, but for the first time in a long time, she didn't want to cross her arms over her chest or search for the light switch.

From the look on his face, Griff didn't want that either. Feeling suddenly bold, Rue slipped out of the rest of her clothes, forcing herself to stand still under his inspection.

He took his time, his gaze trailing from the swell of her breasts, and catching on the glisten between her thighs. She didn't have to read his mind to know he wasn't cataloging her flaws.

Finally, he sat forward, his feet on the ground as if he was planning to stand. She shook her head at him. His eyes darkened when she crawled into his lap instead, pushing him back into the couch, knees pinning him in place.

His hands found her hips, anchoring her roughly against him, but he didn't do more. He kept his head back, searching her eyes, fingers clenching and unclenching at her waist. Waiting for her to take what she wanted.

So she did, tangled her fingers in his hair, tugging his head back for a kiss.

His lips were warm. Wet. He opened his mouth, his tongue tangling with hers. He tasted like desperation.

She rocked against his hardness, nothing between them but the fabric of his pajamas. He groaned underneath her, surging up to chase her mouth as she leaned away. It was a good feeling. Powerful. So she moved again, bracing herself with one hand on his chest as she moved.

He looked up at her, face flush, lips inches from her naked chest. She imagined him on his knees in front of her, and the thought made her smile. Another time.

It must have been the smile that did it, because Griff's patience finally broke. His hands became firm, stopping her from rocking, and he leaned forward to explore her. His lips burned everywhere they touched. His teeth scraped her nipple. His tongue tasted the sweat on her collarbone. His mouth nipped below her ear.

She laughed, delight spiraling out of her, mixing with desire and something else. Something warm and dangerous.

"It's going to be like that, huh?" Griff growled against her jaw.

She cupped his face, kissing him, feeling the sandpaper of his beard underneath her palm. Rubbing her lips raw.

"Maybe," she breathed, pulling off his hoodie and raking her fingernails through the hair on his chest. He shuddered, the hardness caught between her legs twitching in anticipation. She hummed, rocking again and again, until the thin fabric between them was wet.

"Take what you want," he whispered as he lapped at one nipple and then the other. "Please. God."

So she did, slipping her hand beneath the waistband of his pants. He was hot and so hard. She held him, barely moving until he gasped and bucked from the tension—until her fingers were slick. Until her own body throbbed in time with his.

She liked it. Holding him at the precipice. Being the one who decided. But then he begged. A low whisper that made her control falter.

Rue shifted, angling her hips just right. He slid deep inside of her with one smooth stroke. His hands were on her now, pulling her down, swallowing the sound she made with his mouth. She inched her knees forward, taking him deeper, settling in his lap. She held still, kissing the curve of his shoulder, tendrils of heat radiating into ever corner of her body.

The pleasure was too consuming to play with, although she wanted that too, torn between prolonging it and burning it all down. In the end, Griff decided for her. His long fingers slipped between them, touching her where they met. His thumb was rough against her softest flesh, coaxing, as he whispered and swore against her collarbone.

She stopped paying attention to his pleasure, lost in her own as he set a new rhythm, driving up into her in a way that left them both gasping. A shudder ran through her and then another, before they His mouth was on hers and

***

Griff waited nervously outside the bathroom in the dark hallway. The toilet flushed, and he heard the faucet run before the door opened. Rue stepped out, wearing only his hoodie. He couldn't make out her expression. Griff held his breath.

The sex had been fucking amazing. *She* was amazing. And he wanted more. Wanted it right now, if he was honest, but he'd settle for a shy smile or hell, an attaboy pat on the butt—any sign she wasn't going to run.

Rue seemed like a runner. She seemed like the kind of girl who would reconsider things in the light of day. He'd woken up to an empty bed enough times to know her type.

It was the reason he'd held her close when she'd collapsed into his arms, savoring the way the firelight highlighted the freckles on her shoulder. Soaking in the comforting weight of her in his lap as they both spiraled down to earth.

Eventually, she had stirred, kissing him softly before gathering her clothes and disappearing down the hallway without a word. The absence of post-sex banter made him nervous. Suddenly, he wished he'd taken her to bed instead of fucking her in the living room like an animal. At least then they could have dozed off in twisted sheets and maybe even woken tangled together in the morning for a round two.

This, though, was...awkward.

"Hi," Rue said softly, shifting nervously an arm's length away.

"Hi," he told the darkness, searching for something to say that wasn't: *Come to bed with me. I want more.*

There was a pause, as if she was deciding something, and then she drifted into his arms. He breathed into her hair, trying to hold her loosely even though his palms itched to press her tight. He didn't want to scare her.

She smelled like lilacs and sex. Her hand slipped underneath his shirt, resting on the small of his back.

After a moment, she kissed the underside of his jaw and whispered, "Let's go to bed."

He nodded wordlessly, something cracking inside his chest when she took his hand and led him toward his own bedroom. Inside, the moon streaming through the window was the only light. He kept it open an inch, even in the winter, so the crash of the ocean beyond the bluff was a constant lullaby.

She didn't comment on any of it, undressing quietly on the other side of his bed. She left on her underwear before she slipped underneath his rumpled covers, so he did the same. They met in the middle, folding around each other like they'd been sleeping together for years.

"I like your bed," she sighed, snuggling deeper under the fluffy duvet. "I could get used to being rich."

"I put the flannel sheets on last week," he answered. It was a dumb thing to say. Unromantic and painfully normal, as if they were a married couple instead of just lovers, but she didn't seem to notice.

She draped her leg over his, tucked against him so that her breath was soft against his throat. His eyes drifted closed.

He played with her hair, brushing it gently until her breath slowed. Griff thought she'd fallen asleep, but then she shifted, her hand curling on his chest. He reached up, capturing it with his own, and felt the silence change.

"Are you okay?" he whispered, bracing himself for any answer that wasn't Yes.

"It might be the Luck," Rue said quietly, her hand cupped in his. "The feeling you're having right now? It might not be...me."

Griff's eyes opened. The ceiling fan turned slowly overhead. The house creaked. Outside, the ocean muttered and churned.

He searched for something reassuring to say. Something short of "I think I could love you" and far away from "it *does* feel like magic," but the truth was, he didn't know. He'd never felt like this about someone—magical or otherwise—and after a long while, Rue's breathing deepened, and the moment was lost.

Twenty

The bed beside him was empty.

Griff propped himself up on one elbow, studying the expanse of wrinkled sheet where Rue's naked body had been the night before. It was just past dawn, and sunlight created a puddle of light at the end of the bed. A thin layer of fresh snow sparkled outside.

It was the perfect morning to make a woman fall in love with you. He'd planned it before even opening his eyes. Had imagined waking her up with a steaming cup of coffee before pulling her back underneath the covers.

But she was gone. And the sheets beside him were cold.

He held his breath, listening to the house, in case she'd beat him to the coffee, but it was oddly quiet, no dog claws tapping on the hardwood floors or burble of the coffeemaker.

Trying to ignore the uneasy hitch in his chest, he got out of bed, pulling on his clothes before padding down the hallway. He didn't want to jump to conclusions. Maybe Rue was taking Tug out for his morning constitutional or had gotten up to fix them breakfast and was being extra quiet?

There was no one in the kitchen. The coffee pot was empty. The fire from the night before had turned to ash. The blanket on the floor beside the couch was the only sign that last night had even happened.

She was gone.

Griff wasn't sure how he knew, but he did. It was like there was a hollowed-out space in the house that hadn't been there before—an emptiness like haunting. He swallowed the bitterness in the back of his throat and wandered across the cold tile, pushing the button on the coffeemaker. The smell of roasted Ethiopian beans filled the air, but it wasn't as comforting as usual.

He peered out the window, hopeful. Pathetic.

There was no one on the back deck. Not so much as a new footprint in the clean snow—human or dog. Griff checked his phone, but there were no new messages. Reluctantly, he headed for the front door. Her sneakers were missing from the front mat where she'd kicked them off the day before. Only his boots remained.

The hole in his chest widened. A sucker for punishment, Griff slipped his coat on over his pajamas and stepped out onto the porch.

Her car was gone. There were tracks where the Subaru had reversed and headed down the driveway. The snow on the steps was packed down in places. It didn't take Sherlock Holmes to solve this mystery.

Maybe he had missed a note somewhere? Or maybe she'd chased that stupid dog into the woods. He stepped back inside. Tug's leash had been sitting on the bench yesterday, but now it was gone. The hole in his chest ached, but he decided to cover it with righteous anger.

He'd been left before, of course. A dozen times. The bachelor's life is filled with empty morning beds and texts left on READ. He'd seemingly hit it off with women who later blocked him on all socials the very next day.

Rue didn't owe him anything.

Griff closed the front door and went back into the kitchen. He took down his favorite mug and poured his coffee. He made it the way he liked it—cream and sugar—and stood in front of the window.

Maybe it had just been magic after all.

***

Two hours earlier

"We need to get you on a new potty schedule," Rue grumbled, peeling her eyes open.

Tugboat booped her in the cheek again with his cold, wet nose. She batted at the dog blindly in the darkness. At home, she would have squirmed into the middle of the bed, burying her head under the pillow, and ignoring the damn beast, but she didn't want to wake Griff.

Tug easily dodged her flailing hands, resting his chin on the mattress. His tail thumped loudly against the carpet as he waited for her to drag herself out of slumber. Rue sighed. Sometimes she wasn't sure who was in charge around here.

Despite the king-sized bed, Griff's warm body was curled around her spine, one limp arm flopped loosely over her hip. The heavy down comforter was like being enveloped in a soft marshmallow. Rue had never regretted having a dog more. Even in the dark, there was no ignoring the sad eyes staring directly into her soul. tried a few times, shoving Tug away at 4 am and again at 5 am. Apparently, it was an emergency now.

Tug huffed his hot breath directly into her face. His breath smelled like rancid fish.

"Fine," she groaned, shoving him away so she could slip out of the warm covers.

Tug danced happily as she searched the floor for her underwear. They'd mysteriously disappeared sometime in the night. Rue blushed, thinking about the way Griff had woken her, his hands hot on her body. She still had that warm, used, loose feeling that came after good sex.

Tug growled as she pulled on her clothes. It wasn't a real growl, just a low rumble in the back of his throat to signal his dissatisfaction with her current moving speed.

She shushed him, casting a mournful glance at the naked man in the warm bed, as if she wasn't planning on returning to it as soon as her stupid dog had done his business. Griff had rolled onto his stomach. Moonlight danced across the muscles of his back. Rue swore quietly and shooed Tugboat into the hall.

"Traitor," she whispered, following him to the front door. Tug didn't seem concerned, his tail thwapping the wall as she shrugged on her puffy coat and shoved her feet into her wet shoes. She didn't bother bending over to tie the laces. She wasn't planning to be outside for more than three minutes.

Rue clipped on Tug's leash, swung the door open, and groaned. The night sky was clear, pinpricks of stars glowing through the tree branches, but it had snowed, and a dusting of white coated everything. She managed to grab a beanie from the rack before Tug finally got impatient and yanked her outside.

"Damnit!" she yelped, grabbing for the porch railing. Tug, however, charged down the stairs, slipping out of his leash in his enthusiasm. Rue briefly saw her life flash before her eyes when her foot slipped, but somehow made it down the steps without breaking her neck.

Rue held her coat closed with one hand, stomping her feet in the bitter cold as the dog paused to sniff a bush. The tip of her nose tingled.

"Don't even think about running away," she warned, shoving his abandoned collar in her pocket as Tug moved to another tree, sniffing the snowy ground. Suddenly, he wasn't in a hurry.

"If you don't pee soon, I *will* kill you," Rue growled.

Tug looked up at her, ears pricked. She opened her mouth to yell when he barked, one loud ruff that echoed in the darkness.

She shushed him, annoyed, already thinking about slipping back around Griff's warm—

Rue blinked up at the sky. Gravel dug into her back, snow soaking into her hair and coat. The stars were dancing.

Also, she was lying on the ground. Had she slipped?

There were voices. Arguing voices, but her spinning head muffled them. Stunned, she groaned and tried to lift her hand to her temple. Someone stepped on her wrist.

She yelped, tugging at her trapped arm, but the boot resting on it pressed hard. Rue squinted up at the person looming above her, unable to make out a face through the spinning stars. He was big, though. And he was holding a gun.

For three long seconds, the black circle of the muzzle yawned like a black hole, filling her vision. Until Tug yelped.

She'd only heard that sound from him once, when she accidentally stepped on his paw during a drunken Friday night, but even that had been different. This sound had fear laced through it. Rue bolted upright. Nausea swept through her, but she fought it, clawing at the ankle of the man above her.

"Goddamn mutt," the man above her growled, bearing down harder, keeping her trapped.

"I lost him," a woman responded, swearing in another language. "It's fine. Just take her."

This voice, Rue recognized.

Katia.

Twenty-One

The gun pointed at her head had not wavered, although the woman holding it was applying lipstick in the reflection of the car window. Rue shifted uncomfortably for the hundredth time, trying to use the door as leverage to stay upright as the thug driving her Subaru finally pulled off the highway.

She didn't recognize the exit. Her kidnappers had shoved her in the backseat of her own car, her wrists ziptied awkwardly behind her back. Her fingers had fallen asleep hours ago. Or she was guessing it had been hours.

The car turned onto a rural road, passing a sad-looking Wendy's and one of those nondescript gas stations with only two pumps and a window fogged with cigarette smoke. She hadn't gotten a look at the name of the road, but she'd given up on trying to keep track of where they were a while ago. It was hard to pay attention with blood drying on your face.

"Where are we going?" she asked the back of the thug's head, not really expecting an answer. He just grunted.

She'd asked before with the same response, so she decided to try something different. "I need to pee," she tried. It was a long shot, but there was nothing a man feared more than a woman's basic bathroom needs.

The thug didn't even bother to glance in the rearview mirror. He drove the car like it was a luxury vehicle instead of a piece of shit covered in dog hair, the engine straining at the breakneck pace on the highway, and the brakes squealing at all the red lights.

Unfortunately, he wasn't the only other person in the car. Rue glared at the woman next to her, but refused to ask someone holding her at gunpoint any probing questions. She recognized Katia now that she wasn't wearing a scarf and a fur coat. The bitch had been in the market yesterday, reaching for the paprika and doling out advice. Rue wondered how long they had been following her.

Katia certainly looked more recognizable with her hair pulled back into an elegant chignon, but her mascara was smudged from the scuffle in the snow, a detail that gave Rue great pleasure. The thug had been the one to grab her outside Griff's house, but it had been Katia who held the gun to her temple.

Rue had been too busy talking to Tug about his morning bathroom habits even to notice the dark sedan parked behind her car in Griff's driveway. All she'd been thinking about was the warm man she'd left behind in the bed.

Tug barked once more, before the bag fell over her head, a deep woof that had startled her into looking up, but by then it was too late.

She wasn't mad at him. She might not be in this situation if she'd rescued a German Shepard instead of a long-legged coward, but at least Tug had warned her enough to knock the syringe out of Katia's hand before they tossed her in the back seat like a trussed chicken. Rue didn't know what had been in that needle, but considering the bitch's unhappy sneer when it shattered in the snow, she was glad it wasn't in her bloodstream.

At least her stupid dog was okay. Sometime during the ensuing struggle, he had fled into the woods.

Rue shifted again, half lying across the back seat in an attempt to feel her hands again.

"You know, this Luck thing only works if I'm happy. Comfortable," she said, gritting her teeth as a spike of pain lanced between her shoulder blades.

This was a lie. For all she knew, her dead body would be lucky.

Katia turned to her, one thin eyebrow raised. The muzzle of the tiny silver gun balanced on top of her designer purse didn't move. "You don't strike me as a happy person, darling."

"Same, bitch," Rue snapped. The last thing she needed right now was to be psychoanalyzed by a damn criminal.

Katia shrugged and pulled out her phone, somehow tapping out a long text. "You will be comfortable. We are almost at our destination."

She sagged back against the seat. They had passed a few run-down strip malls after turning off the freeway, but now there were fields on either side for miles, empty and snow-covered.

Rue knew what Griff was going to find when he woke up to an empty bed. She'd done her fair share of sneaking out of Hinge date apartments. She knew the walk of shame intimately, not to mention the awkward "hey, it was fun, but you're not for me," text that inevitably followed. Griff had no way to know that this morning was any different.

Which meant she was on her own. The thought made her heart hurt.

The empty fields eventually gave way to a long chain-link fence. A strip of asphalt appeared behind it, lined with red blinking lights. Half a dozen small prop planes were parked in the grass nearby. The only sign of life was the fluttering orange cone flag attached to the squat concrete building beside the runway.

Rue straightened. An airport.

Don't turn here.

As if he heard her, the thug put on his blinker.

"Fuck," she muttered.

Katia smirked and started gathering her things. "Ah, now the girl sees."

"What do you want with me?" Rue snapped, refusing to give the woman the gift of her fear.

Katia shrugged, the dainty gun still balanced on her lap. She didn't answer, and Rue didn't expect her to.

There were two other cars parked in the gravel lot beside the concrete building: a pristine black sedan with tinted windows and a beat-up Honda hatchback decorated with a dozen bumper stickers, including one with the slogan, "I LIKE TO GET HIGH."

A sleek jet idled on the runway, Steam rising from the warming engines. For the first time since Katia had put a gun to her head, Rue felt something other than annoyance about her current situation.

She tugged at the zip ties as they parked, but all that did was make her wrists ache. She'd seen TikToks on how to break through them. What was it? Make them tight around your wrists and then jerk back towards—

"Don't even think about it," the thug growled, swinging open her door and yanking her out of the car. A large gun peeked out of his jacket, but he didn't bother pulling it. She wasn't dangerous.

But she could be annoying. Rue dragged her feet as they crossed the parking lot until the thug squeezed her bicep so hard she squeaked in pain.

There was no stopping their march to the plane. She considered dropping something, like a pathetic fairytale Gretel, but she had nothing but an old cough drop wrapper in her pocket, and she doubted even the most talented detective was going to deduce much from that.

Rue caught a glimpse of the Honda owner standing beside the concrete building as the thug forced her up the jet's narrow stairs, his hand raised to shade his eyes as he watched them board. In a wrinkled tie-dye shirt and faded Seahawks ball cap, he looked more like a gamer than a plane operator.

"He won't save you," the thug hissed in her ear. "Carl is well paid for his blindness."

Rue smiled sweetly over her shoulder. "Carl can eat my ass."

***

Griff was pouring cereal at the kitchen counter when Sarah finally came out of her room. The oven clock said it was 8:14 am. She shuffled to the coffee pot, yawning and rubbing at the rat's nest she called hair as she poured a cup.

"You're up early," he said gruffly. He wasn't normally chatty in the morning, but he'd do anything to cut the morose silence, even endure small talk with his sister.

Sarah crossed to the fridge, pulled out a jug of hazelnut creamer, and poured an insane amount into her coffee. He grimaced.

"The damn dog woke me up whining at the front door," she said, taking a sip. Griff looked down at Turnip, who had somehow managed to thread his thick body between the feet of the stool. He was snoring.

"Dog?" Griff said, adding milk to his bowl.

Sarah took a sip of her coffee, wrinkled her nose, and added more creamer. "Yeah, you need to talk to your girlfriend. What kind of houseguest shoves her dog outside at bumfuck in the morning and leaves him out there in the cold?"

Griff's cereal spoon hovered mid-air. He frowned. "Sarah. Rue left."

Sarah's head tilted. "Left? What? Where? I assumed you two were going at it like rabbits this morning."

The stool screeched as he pushed it back, interrupting Turnip's nap. "Did you say Tug's outside?"

He didn't wait for an answer, heading down the hallway. Suddenly, there was something else inside his chest other than a bitter hole. He swallowed, shoving his feet into his boots.

Sarah trailed after him with her mug. "Rue left? What the hell did you do?"

Griff ignored her, swinging open the front door. Tug burst inside, bringing along a gust of cold air. He raced down the hallway to Sarah and then made an abrupt U-turn, pulling up a corner of the runner, before bounding back to Griff. He left big, wet footprints behind him. His collar was gone.

Turnip sat on his haunches beside Sarah, looking bewildered by all the commotion. Frantic, Tug did a tight loop around Griff, shivering all over, before running back to Sarah. He finally came to a trembling stop in front of her.

A twig was snarled in one of his soft ears. She knelt, putting her coffee mug on the floor, and gently extracted it.

"It's okay, boy," she murmured, running her hands across his trembling body. Tug whined.

"Is he hurt?" Griff asked gruffly. His whole body was cold, and it didn't have anything to do with the open door.

"You said she left?" Sarah asked, looking up at him. "When was this?"

He spread his palms, sick with guilt. "An hour ago? I thought she bailed, Sarah! Ghosted. You know, like girls do sometimes! Her car was gone, and..."

Sarah pulled Tug into a full-body hug. They both looked up at him with accusatory eyes. Griff's stomach bottomed out.

Fuck.

"You thought the girl who voluntarily helped us twice after you fucking kidnapped her, split before dawn because of some relationship drama despite the millions of dollars on the line?" Sarah asked slowly.

Hearing it out loud made it sound as stupid as it was.

Griff swore, slamming the door shut and barging past her toward the bedroom. "Where would she go?"

Sarah shook her head, following him. "I don't know. But I've got a bad feeling. Who even knew she was here?"

Griff's mind whirled. The bedroom was as he left it, sheets askew. The only sign of Rue was her phone, sitting dark on the side table. Sarah saw it at the same time he did. Her face dropped.

There was one person who knew who Rue Adler might be.

Sarah stood on the other side of the bed, one hand still on Tug's wet head. The dog looked eagerly between them, waiting for the dumb humans to figure out what he already knew.

"Grant Reddington," Sarah said, and it wasn't a question.

Griff nodded grimly. "Grant Reddington."

Twenty-Two

"Well, if it isn't my Lucky Penny! Welcome!"

Grant Reddington clapped his hands together as the thug pushed her down the jet's aisle, as if this were a vacation and not a crime. Rue guessed every day was a vacation when you were a millionaire.

Grant was certainly dressed the part, in a pale linen suit and leather flip-flops; he looked exactly like the rich asshole he was. Rue did not doubt that the watch glinting on his wrist cost more than her yearly salary.

"What is this?" she snapped, although she already had a pretty good idea.

Grant pouted at her over his glass of white wine. "There's no need for hostility. I have a business proposition."

"Email exists, you asshole."

The thug shoved her into the plush seat across from his boss. It was more like an expensive armchair than anything you'd typically find in an airplane. The cushion hissed quietly as she sank into it, and the leather felt like it was made from the skin of baby lambs. Even the air inside the jet smelled nice, like lavender and wealth, instead of disinfectant and bad coffee.

Grant's thug leaned over her, snapping the zip ties that bound her hands with an unnecessarily large knife, but not before buckling her tightly into the seat. He turned his head as he did it, his meaty face inches from hers.

"This is a locked seatbelt," he growled. "You will be secure for the duration of the flight."

She showed him her teeth. "Your breath smells like ham."

His beady eyes narrowed, but he knew his place and left to take a seat two rows away next to Katia on the other end of the jet. Near enough to give his boss privacy, but close enough keep an eye on her.

The only other passenger was a beautiful young woman with flaming red hair and the shortest skirt Rue had ever seen. Red hair didn't even bother looking up; her bare thighs crossed as she thumbed through her phone, head bobbing to whatever pop music was no doubt played in her headphones.

"Would you like a drink, my dear?" Grant smiled, setting his glass down with a clink, as if she were a guest and not a prisoner. Rue ignored him.

She'd never been on a private jet, but it was exactly like the movies. Cream armchairs faced each other over small marble tables bolted to the floor. Classical music played quietly overhead, and the space was lit with soft, pleasant lighting. The carpet was so white it looked as if it had been installed the night before. She understood now why they'd confiscated her muddy shoes at the door and exchanged them for soft slippers. She was a long way from economy.

Aside from the small group of passengers, there seemed to be a single flight attendant, who was busy doing something with ice in the back of the plane. The door to the cockpit was already shut tight.

Rue shifted experimentally against the seat belt, but it cinched tighter every time she moved. Outside the small window, there was nothing but a field of dead grass.

Grant studied her as the jet hummed to life around them. "Look at me, Penny."

"That's not my fucking name," she answered, keeping her eyes on the pitted stretch of pavement acting as a runway.

He waved a hand as if her actual name was of no consequence. "You're hardly in a position to assert your will, my dear."

Rue glared down at her lap, teeth grinding. The plane rocked into motion. There was no way she was doing anything this maniac asked her to do.

Grant glanced over his shoulder at the thug. "Benson, would you mind?"

Benson didn't bother rising from his seat as the plane taxied. He opened his sports jacket, flashing the butt of the massive gun secured in his holster. The message was clear.

"You like to be in control," Rue observed, glaring at Grant's smug face.

"I do," he replied pleasantly, gesturing toward the flight attendant with his empty glass. "I've come to expect it, in fact."

The attendant rushed over. She was petite and young. Her name tag read Ashley Chen, and she wore a crisp navy-blue uniform over a tight pencil skirt. She wasn't wearing a bra, which Rue knew because her fitted blazer gapped around her small chest when she bent to refill Grant's glass.

Grant patted her hip, smiling straight into the woman's cleavage. "Bring our guest a water, will you, darling? In a sealed plastic bottle."

The flight attendant nodded before scurrying away. Rue wrinkled her nose.

The engine revved , and the pilot came on the overhead to announce that they were about to take off. Rue gave her belt a test tug before surrendering fully to the soft seat. Wherever this plane was going, she was going with it.

"Tell me, love, do you think a man such as myself likes being taken for a fool?" Grant asked.

Rue watched the runway rumble by, slowly, and then faster as the plane picked up speed. "This is about Griff, isn't it?"

Grant shrugged one shoulder. "He took something from me."

She waved at the jet. "You *have* plenty, don't you think?"

"Never, dear little Penny. Never."

Her stomach dropped as the plane lifted off the ground. She watched for a minute as they cut above the clouds and banked to the left, trying to guess where they were going. "The girl then? Candi? Is this about her?"

Grant looked confused for a moment, as if he had forgotten Sarah even existed, and then he laughed. "Goodness, you are a hoot. No, I have a dozen girls just like Candi, who will lap at my feet if I say the word."

"Ew."

The plane leveled out. The coastline came into view on the horizon. There had been no passport check, so she assumed they were going somewhere domestic, which was a relief.

"So?" Rue asked, still gripping the armrests. "What *is* this about?"

Grant adjusted his silver cufflinks. They matched the gray hair at his temples. "Dignity, Penny. This is about dignity."

***

The copilot wasn't dead.

Griff had checked his pulse (slow and steady) and breathing (deep) before awkwardly stashing his body behind the seats. It was a tight fit because of the jet's small cockpit, but he'd managed to stow the unconscious man underneath some flight jackets and the pilot's lunch box.

He could hear the murmur of voices behind him, on the other side of the locked cockpit door. His heart thumped. He'd barely made it in time. It had been a race since Sarah had unlocked Rue's phone (with the code: 1-2-3-4, of course) and discovered the moving blip in her location settings. Thank god for the airtag in Tug's lost collar or all would be lost.

As it was, he had to guess where they were taking her as he pushed his BMW's speed to the limit. Grant's private airfield had seemed like a good bet, but he'd barely gotten slipped onto the warming jet before Rue's car pulled into gravel parking lot.

Griff buckled himself into the copilot's abandoned seat, wondered if the woman who'd packed the lunch box knew her husband was moonlighting for very bad people. He guessed not. Women tended to be smarter than that. Besides, Mr. Pilot wasn't wearing a wedding ring.

He was young for someone in charge of an aircraft—maybe late twenties—with an overgrown blond crew cut that made Griff think he was probably ex-military. The man was wearing the standard pilot uniform, right down to the polished black shoes and the flight wings pinned to his suit jacket, but everything was wrinkled, and he had a 5 o'clock shadow that was rapidly becoming a 6 o'clock shadow. His name tag said "Benji Johnson."

Benji side-eyed him and then reached over to push one of the many blinking buttons on the console. His hand trembled. It would have been a normal response to having your coworker knocked unconscious and your plane hijacked, but good old Benji's hands had already been unsteady when Griff had slipped into the cockpit and tapped his co-pilot behind the ear with the butt of his gun.

The two men hadn't even noticed the door slide open behind them. They'd been arguing—angry, hushed whispers that Griff guessed had everything to do with Benji's red-rimmed eyes. He suspected that Benji packed his own lunch. Things that were most certainly not a ham sandwich (i.e., Coke or pills), which wasn't a comforting thought as they accelerated down the runway, so he kept quiet until the jet lifted off the ground. He wanted coked-up Benji to concentrate.

"So," Griff said cheerfully, once they'd reached cruising altitude. It had been a surprisingly smooth take-off considering the driver. "Here's what's going to happen."

"Please don't kill us," Benji said, his shaking hand settling on what Griff assumed was the throttle.

Griff slapped him on the shoulder. Benji flinched. "How about we make a deal? I won't kill us if you don't kill us. How's that?"

Benji nodded reluctantly, reaching up to adjust a button above his head. Despite his shifty eyes, the plane stayed steady, buzzing toward the horizon as if a drunk wasn't at the helm. Technology really was amazing.

"What do you want me to do?" Benji asked, his thin lips pressed tight as if he was considering puking. He had a boyish face underneath his unkempt scruff and pale blue eyes that would have been more suited to a beach bum than someone operating a million-dollar jet.

Griff studied the controls, but couldn't decipher anything. Everything he knew about flying was from video games. He needed Benji.

"Where are we heading?" Griff asked, ignoring the question.

Benji swallowed. "Private airstrip in Kauai."

Griff lifted an eyebrow. The Pacific Ocean loomed past the nose of the plane as they glided over dense pine forest. It certainly *looked* like Benji was telling the truth. He shouldn't have been surprised. Grant Reddington owned numerous houses. Five to be exact. But this particular one was well hidden behind a tax shelter and a shell corporation.

He had dug up the dirty little secret while doing his poker research. Grant had the slimy sheen of new money because he'd made his first few million counting cards at every high-rolling table across the continent, which was fine if the man hadn't continued his quest to become stinking rich by dabbling in human trafficking and drugs. The name he flaunted wasn't even his own. He'd been born Ricky Jenson in a tiny town in the Piedmont of North Carolina, whose claim to fame was the stinky paper factory and two (two!) Dollar Trees. Everything about the man was a lie.

"How often do you fly our rich bastard out there?" Griff asked, stretching out his legs the best he could in the narrow cockpit and trying not to bump anything that looked important.

Benji licked his lips, glancing down at the to-go coffee in the cup holder, but didn't reach for it. "I'm his primary pilot...but there are others."

Griff huffed. "I'm sure. Tell me, Benji—why *are* you so damn shaky?"

For the first time, Benji's bloodshot eyes flashed with something more than fear. At least the man had a little fire left in him.

"I think it's pretty obvious," he responded, grimly, reaching for his coffee. At least the man wasn't a liar, Griff thought. There wasn't anything worse than someone who didn't know they were a disaster.

Griff crossed his ankles, watching the clouds roll by outside. "Grant keeps you pretty comfortable financially, I'd guess. You aren't thinking about pushing some secret button or anything?"

Benji's jaw twitched. "No."

He'd never heard a less convincing bluff. Benji had eyed the console suspiciously several times since they took off, and even though he didn't know shit about flying, Griff recognized the radio that would contact air traffic control. And the authorities.

Griff pulled his phone from his pocket. The photo was the first thing that popped up. He handed it over to the young pilot. Benji's eyes widened. It was a selfie Sarah had taken in front of Benji's parents' house. She was sitting in the old truck, looking tired despite the grin and thumbs up she was mugging for the camera. It didn't take a genius to notice Griff's spare rifle balanced on the dashboard behind her.

Benji paled, handing back the phone stiffly.

Griff hated to see the man's rebellion fade, but he had places to be. "You see, Benji, I have insurance. In case you inconveniently get your bravery back during our little flight."

"Don't hurt them," Benji rasped.

He wasn't going to. Sarah had talked to Benji's mother at her mailbox while walking Tug and reported back that Betsy was a lovely retired nurse who liked knitting and ran a murder mystery book club in her spare time.

Griff wasn't in the business of hurting innocent people, no matter what their shit son was up to in his spare time. But good 'ole Benji didn't know that.

Twenty-Three

The door to paradise was locked. Rue tried the doorknob again, jiggling it in case she'd been too stupid and exhausted to figure it out last night, but it remained firmly secure.

Her prison door was at least ten feet tall, made of dark, aged wood, and was every bit as opulent as the rest of Grant's estate. She'd only caught glimpses when Benson hustled her inside. They'd passed through a massive, open-air living space where tropical plants mingled with leather couches and thick rugs, an elegant hybrid of traditional Hawaiian style—thatch and stone. She'd gotten an impression of the dark ocean just past a manicured lawn before being swept upstairs and into this locked bedroom.

Rue studied the heavy bronze doorknob for signs that it could be picked by an amateur, but it was clearly handcrafted, the handle intricately carved into the shape of a damn peacock. The king-sized bed behind her had been made up with crisp white sheets in a thread count she couldn't even fathom. Mosquito netting fluttered around the teak canopy frame. She'd only managed to defiantly resist its soft mattress for a few minutes last night before tipping onto the feather pillows and falling into a coma.

After seven hours in the air and a night with more sex than sleep, she'd been dead on her feet. The bedding smelled like orange blossoms. Rue wouldn't have admitted to Grant under knife point that she'd had a deliriously fantastic sleep or that she'd lifted the corner of the mattress this morning to find out the brand.

Rue leaned against the locked door and eyed the bamboo tray someone had slipped onto the dresser while she slept, which was creepy as fuck, but the smell of coffee wafting up from the silver carafe made her mouth water. She hesitated for only a minute (poison? sleeping potions?) before pouring herself a cup.

It was delicious, damn it.

Beside the carafe, a delicate china bowl overflowed with freshly cut tropical fruit, mango, papaya, and pineapple. Reluctantly, she peeked under the linen napkin covering a second bowl and discovered a basket of warm, hole-less donuts .

She was a terrible prisoner. A good one would go on a hunger strike and pound on the door until someone came, but it had been at least a year since her dinner last night, and she was lightheaded. Rue picked up the donut and took a bite. All thoughts of being a "good" prisoner disappeared. The donut was filled with warm passionfruit jelly. Her eyes rolled, and she grabbed another, ignoring the blizzard of powdered sugar suddenly coating the front of her pajamas.

Yes, she'd changed into the unbearably soft pajamas Grant had left out on the foot of the bed. Was it a crime to be clean and comfortable?

Rue cursed herself and ate another donut. This was definitely the best kidnapping she'd ever experienced, which was saying a lot considering that the last one involved a man who kissed like a dream. She plucked a slice of mango from the bowl and padded over to the balcony, grumbling to herself. The fruit was almost as good as the damn pastry.

She'd been surprised to find the balcony door unlocked, but the bedroom was on the third floor, and at least thirty feet off the ground.

Rue leaned against the railing and gazed out over the ocean just beyond a line of rustling palms. It was exactly the opposite of the angry darkness roaring off Griff's back deck. This version of the Pacific was calm and clear and so turquoise that she had to squint. A small white sand beach curved past the lawn, tasteful lounge chairs tucked beneath the trees, pale yellow umbrellas fluttering an invitation.

Along the coastline, there wasn't another house in sight, no matter how far she leaned over the railing. Rue didn't know much about Hawaiian politics, but she suspected the native population was not too happy about giving up a piece of their paradise to a mainlander—especially one like Grant Reddington.

Rue popped the last piece of mango into her mouth. It tasted like flowers, sweet and meltingly soft. She should look for a way to escape. Just because this was the most beautiful place she'd ever seen didn't mean she should just lie back and enjoy the view. Right?

She peered over the railing. There was grass beneath her, but it didn't look soft enough to cushion a fall from so high up, and there were no conveniently placed footholds or ivy along the stone wall as there would be in a movie. There was, however, another balcony beside her own.

It was about three feet away and would have been entirely out of reach if it weren't for the decorative ledge connecting them. Rue's stomach wobbled. Ledge was a generous term for the piece of trim connecting the two balconies. She couldn't measure, but the strip couldn't have been more than four inches wide. Her foot would fit on it, but just barely.

"Don't be crazy," she muttered. Even if she somehow managed to swing herself across the gap to the next balcony, there was no guarantee that the door would be unlocked. Or unguarded.

"It's just a few feet," she said louder, trying to hype herself up.

Her stomach lurched. Herself wasn't listening.

Rue headed back inside. She ate the rest of her breakfast on top of the impossibly white duvet before heading to the shower. If she was going to attempt death-defying hijinks, she might as well be clean, she thought.

The bathroom was as impressive as the rest of the house, with white subway tile and a jungle of tropical plants that enhanced the rich green wallpaper. Rue glanced longingly at the claw-foot bathtub that sat in front of a window overlooking the ocean before stepping into the shower. She didn't have time for a soak, even if the glass jar of bubble bath at the end of the tub smelled like jasmine.

Afterward, wrapped in a fluffy towel, she took advantage of the mahogany wardrobe in the bedroom. It was filled with tag-on designer clothes that seemed to have been ordered specifically to her measurements. Grant was an asshole, but he was a classy asshole.

Rue wouldn't admit to anyone that she tried on a pretty sundress decorated with tiny white flowers before opting for a more practical escaping-from-a-psycho outfit. The breeze off the ocean kept the house cool, but the temperature outside was climbing, so she chose a loose white blouse and a pair of linen pants before securing her damp hair into a practical braid.

She stood in the center of the room with her hands on her hips. She'd half hoped that Benson or Katia would appear to interrupt her stupid plan, but there hadn't been so much as a peep from behind the mahogany door. She sighed. At least her underwear would be clean when they carted her pancake-shaped body off in the ambulance.

Rue stepped back outside. The pinks of sunrise had faded, and the sky was squintingly blue. There was no one in sight—not a stray gardener or housekeeper that she could signal to for help. She was certain it was not a coincidence.

The ledge had, impossibly, shrunk while she showered.

Rue climbed over the railing anyway, swinging one leg over before lowering herself slowly, prodding for the narrow ledge with one bare foot. She'd decided on no shoes for her escape, but she'd tied a pair of sneakers together by the laces. They dangled from her neck awkwardly.

She grazed the ledge with her toes and then swung the rest of the way over, her biceps trembling as she lowered her full weight onto the narrow strip of wood. Her left foot dangled over nothing.

"This is stupid," she said, trying not to look down and failing. The perfectly manicured grass below her was a mile away.

Her hands turned to claws, fixed around the railing. Rue glared at them, heart racing, and tried to convince them to move as sweat trickled down her back, plastering the white blouse to her spine. The ocean murmured. The air smelled like damn orange blossoms. Now was not the time to freak out, Rue scolded her brain as her left foot dangled.

This is exactly the right time to freak out, her brain responded.

Which was fair.

Rue took a deep breath, trying to calm her racing heart. Her right hip was pressed firmly against the building's outside wall, and her right foot was secure on the ledge. All she had to do was pirouette and grab hold of the other balcony in one smooth movement. Easy peasy.

Rue swallowed. One, two, three...

Nope.

She was still clinging to her own railing, knuckles white. A breeze ruffled the bits of hair that had already come loose from her braid, but there was no way to brush them from her eyes. Her stomach swooped as the hint of wind rustled the palm trees, her brain suddenly convinced the flutter was the beginning of a hurricane that would blow her off the side of the house.

Her right thigh started to tremble from holding her up, and she suddenly regretted her unused Planet Fitness membership with all her heart. Her breath was coming fast now, short puffs that darkened the edge of her vision. There were only two options: climb back into her beautiful prison or climb out.

Fuck.

Grimly, Rue blinked back the darkness and spun before she could let herself think about it any longer, forcing herself to let go. She wobbled, her foot slipping a centimeter before her hands landed on the railing of the other balcony. Her thigh muscle twitched again, but she didn't fall. Her right foot, however, had landed crookedly on the ledge. She gasped, hurled herself over the railing, and collapsed in a heap on the balcony.

She stared up at the blue sky, trying to calm her breath. Thankfully, there were curtains across the balcony door, hiding her escapades from view. There was still no one on the lawn or the white sand beach. Grant's attempt to keep her hidden was working in her favor.

After a few breaths, Rue stood, legs still trembling, and pressed her ear to the balcony door . There was no sound or light from the room.

She eased open the door and peeked inside. It was dark—a bedroom, almost identical to the one she had left. Someone had kicked off a pair of black heels at the foot of the bed, and a dress was draped over the desk chair. A bamboo breakfast tray sat on the dresser, a twin to the one delivered to her room. It looked untouched.

Someone had clearly been here. And recently.

Rue slipped inside the room, wincing as the balcony door snicked closed behind her. She pressed herself against the wall, getting a brief impression of pale blue wallpaper and a painting that looked suspiciously like one of Monet's water lilies, when someone bolted upright in the bed.

"How the hell did you get in here?" the stranger demanded.

Twenty-Four

Once they landed in Kauai, it didn't take much convincing to get Benji to fly back to the mainland without his boss. Griff just showed the pilot a selfie of Sarah eating a bowl of Frosted Flakes in his parents' living room. Apparently, Tracy and Fred kept the house key under the mat and attended water aerobics every Tuesday morning.

Benji even called him an Uber before taxiing back to the runway and disappearing into the clouds.

Twenty minutes later, Griff stood at Grant's doorstep. The man's 3rd vacation home was no less lavish than his primary residence, although this one was built with pale stucco walls, volcanic stone pathways, and a massive thatched roof that must have cost a fortune.

This time, Griff didn't bother knocking on Grant's door before going inside. There were plenty of cameras following his arrival, but either no one was watching them, or it was too early for visitors because even Grant's bodyguard looked surprised when Griff strolled onto the back patio.

The bodyguard rose from his chair, reaching for his side piece, but Grant glanced up at Griff calmly through his bifocals while folding his newspaper. Who reads a fucking newspaper these days? A pretentious prick, that's who.

The bodyguard flicked off the snap securing his gun, but Grant just waved a hand. "Benson, be a dear and get our guest a cup of coffee?"

Benson hesitated, his hand still on his weapon. His expression shifted to subdued outrage. Griff guessed being treated like waitstaff hadn't been on his bucket list when he was discharged from whatever branch of the military he'd left.

Grant, oblivious to Benson's existential crisis, turned his head slightly at the delay and lifted an eyebrow. The bodyguard's lips flattened, but he spun on his heel and stalked away.

The billionaire took a sip from his tiny espresso cup. There was enough food on the table in front of him to feed a family of six, including a heaping bowl of freshly sliced mango, a pile of soft rolls covered in sugar, and a platter of smoked salmon sprinkled with capers and red onion. Griff doubted the man ate any of it. Grant struck him as a wheatgrass smoothie kind of asshole.

Grant crossed one ankle onto his knee. He was wearing loafers without socks and a white linen shirt. He looked like a damn Bond villain, one arm dropped over the back of his chair.

"What a not-entirely-unexpected surprise, Mr. Banks," Grant said, clearly amused. He put down his cup with a click and gestured at the chair beside him. Griff pulled out the chair at the opposite end of the table instead. He smelled bad from eight hours of plane travel, and his clothes were hopelessly wrinkled, but he'd "borrowed" Benji's sunglasses and kept them firmly in place as he sat down. It wasn't the best armor, but it would have to do.

"You took something of mine," Griff said, keeping his expression mild even though he wanted to punch the smug look from Grant's damn face.

"I didn't know you were in the business of owning people, too," Grant said, tilting his head in mock curiosity.

Griff's stomach turned. The mansion's patio was more of a tropical grotto, complete with a glimmering pool, burbling waterfall, and a stunning slice of the blue ocean. The surrounding palm trees rustled above a large hot tub, and there was a rack of gleaming, unused surfboards against the house that must have cost a fortune. He knew exactly how Grant afforded his lavish lifestyle, and it wasn't poker.

"I've already notified the authorities about Rue," Griff lied. "I doubt you want that kind of attention considering your current, uh, business activities."

"Boring. I thought you'd be a little more fun, given your complicated hobbies." He plucked a slice of papaya from a bowl and sighed. "And I'll call that bluff. The young lady hasn't even been missing twenty-four hours, and you aren't a notify-the-authorities kind of man."

Griff kept his face blank, crossing his legs and staring out over the ocean as if this wasn't one of the most important bluffs of his life. He shrugged. "Okay. I'll sweeten the pot. I have something of yours, too."

This, finally, made Grant pause. He looked over the top of his glasses. "Oh?"

"Let's just say, Benji was very helpful."

It took a minute. Grant wasn't exactly the kind of guy to keep a mental record of his staff, but Griff saw when the realization swept over him. He burst out laughing.

"Well, touché, my young friend—perhaps you aren't as boring as I had feared." He took off his glasses, swiping under his eyes as the laughter tapered to chuckles. "The jet. Of course!"

Griff hated that he understood Grant's reaction to losing a 15-million-dollar jet. Despite what was at stake, there was a secret glee at being outsmarted. A twisted relief that someone else might be more morally corrupt than you.

The thought made him feel gross. Suddenly, he wanted to be as far away from this asshole and anything they had in common as possible.

Grant threaded his fingers together. "What do you propose? Your Lucky Penny is quite the commodity."

Griff grit his teeth at the nickname but let it pass. "I propose another game. No cheating. No limits."

"Stakes?"

"The jet in exchange for Rue."

Grant's smile faded, and he waved a hand. "I'll just buy another plane. I fear your lucky charm is priceless. Even if she's kinda a bitch."

Griff was saved from saying anything to ruin the deal when Benson appeared, holding a delicate cup of coffee in his meaty paws. He trudged over, setting it on the table with a clatter. A third of it spilled into the saucer. It smelled heavenly.

"What do you want?" he asked.

Grant grinned, opening his arms wide. "Everything."

Griff's heart sank. He'd have to sacrifice everything to get Rue away from this monster—his house, his savings, his whole life. It was a bad bet. No reasonably successful poker player would even consider it.

He sighed. "Done."

***

There was a naked woman underneath the maybe-Monet. Two, actually.

The redhead clutched the sheet to her chin and stared at Rue in astonishment. She was petite, with porcelain skin that looked like it belonged on a magazine cover. The silk sheets pooled in her lap. She couldn't have been more than nineteen. It took Rue a minute to place her without her clothes, but then she remembered the beautiful young woman scrunched next to Benson on the plane—the one with the headphones and the bored expression.

She didn't look bored now.

"How did you get in here?" she hissed, clearly trying not to wake the naked woman sleeping beside her.

The second woman was Katia. Rue would have recognized her dark bob and delicate frame anywhere, even sprawled face down across silk sheets. One perfect butt cheek was exposed, her leg hitched into an L as she slept.

It didn't take a genius to figure out what was happening here. The room still smelled like sex, and the redhead hadn't bothered reaching for her phone, which was charging on the nightstand.

Rue's shoulders relaxed. Finally, luck was breaking her way. This little affair clearly wasn't Grant-approved.

"Get out," the girl mouthed, her cheeks and chest flushing. She glanced nervously at Katia's still body and then the door as if she could make Rue leave with her eyes.

Rue didn't have to be asked twice. If Katia woke, there was no telling what kind of chaos would ensue, regardless of what shenanigans were happening behind Grant's back. She crossed the room swiftly and slipped out the door. She'd expected the hallway to be full of Benson, but it was empty except for a marble bust of Grant, lit tastefully on a pedestal.

She didn't have time to make fun of the statue, even in her mind. There was every chance that the redhead would come to her senses any second and reach for her phone. Or the thug would turn the corner on his way to take a shit. Rue cocked her head, listening to the quiet house as she fumbled with the shoes tied around her neck.

Rue could hear the low murmur of voices from somewhere outside. She didn't try to identify them. There was no time. She slipped on the sneakers and ran, her footsteps muted by the thick carpet. She was surprised when she made it down the grand stair-case to the living room without being seen, surprised when the front door opened easily, and when she skidded to a stop on the pebble driveway. Behind her, the red eye of a camera watched from the eaves.

The driveway was long, disappearing through thick trees before vanishing around a corner. She couldn't hear any traffic, and there was no telling how far she was from civilization. Rue swore quietly. She should have paid more attention during the drive from the airstrip, but she'd fallen asleep.

Around the estate, lush green mountains rose steeply on all sides. Rue even spotted a waterfall, high and thin and caught in the clouds. They must be miles from town.

A bright red jeep was parked in the driveway. Grant didn't strike her as the off-roading type, and the paint was spotless. It didn't have any doors, but after a frantic search, it was clear the key wasn't stashed in the visor or under the mat. The only hot-wiring she knew was from action movies.

She was running out of options. The red eye blinked. Through the palms, the ocean twinkled invitingly. Maybe it wasn't the best choice, but at least she would die somewhere pretty. Rue turned toward it and ran.

Twenty-Five

The poker game went deep into the night. Eventually, they ended up in Grant's game room, a round turret at the top of his estate with a spectacular view of the ocean. A poker table dominated the space. The only other furniture was a gilded sideboard lined with top shelf liquor.

Griff had checked the room thoroughly, looking for the double mirrors, hidden drawers, and secret buttons that the rich were known to hide in their private game rooms. No one liked winning more than those who already had, but he was surprised to find it clean.

"Unlike you, I'm no cheat," Grant had said, watching him search from the doorway with crossed arms and a martini glass. Griff hadn't had a comeback for that, because it wasn't a lie.

He'd always been proud of winning on his own merit—until Sarah. It turned out your moral code was only as solid as the stakes you were willing to wager. Did cheating once make you a cheater? Even if it was for a good reason?

Now, hours later, Griff cast aside the question and forced himself to focus on the game. The chips in front of him had slowly dwindled as the night wore on. He tapped the corner of his cards on the table, his poker face no doubt wavering.

This was the last hand, and it wasn't looking good. His eyes were gritty, and his lower back ached from sitting for so long. Turns out a cockpit is not the greatest place for a restful nap, and the night before had been filled with Rue. It seemed like a million years ago.

Even now, he didn't regret waking her before the sun rose for a second round, though. She'd been too warm to resist, her head tucked underneath his chin, as if it belonged there. It had been softer than the first time, so slow and lazy he'd almost thought it had been a dream when he woke up hours later to find his bed empty.

God, he'd fucked up.

Griff glanced again at his cards. A pair of eights. Hardly a winning hand.

Across the table, Grant looked fresh as a daisy if you didn't count the loosened tie and the empty martini glass at his elbow.

At some point, the redhead Griff had spotted disembarking the jet from his hiding place in the cockpit, had wandered into the room to sit on Grant's lap. She'd kissed his neck, murmuring in his ear and rubbing his thigh while they played, but eventually she got bored. Now it was just Katia, looking like a marble statue as she stood by the dark window with a glass of wine.

Grant turned the river card (A Jack of clubs. Not helpful), contemplated his hand, and then pushed a large stack of chips into the center of the table. Griff counted silently, although the wolf of a smile on the asshole's face was enough clue to know it was a knockout punch.

He barely managed to keep his face still. It turned out that he'd been right to cheat the first time. He'd underestimated Grant's skill as a card player, assuming that he was just a bored man with deep pockets. But it turned out even a rich man could have real talent.

The panic that he'd been keeping at bay suddenly threatened to choke him. Every chip he tossed in the pile was a piece of the life he'd carefully built. His home and his private surfing cove. His beloved truck and fancy espresso machine. The nest egg hiding in an offshore account.

All for a girl he'd slept with once. It was easily the stupidest thing he'd ever done.

"Just fold, my friend. End this with some dignity," Grant said softly, sensing weakness like a circling shark. Griff didn't bother answering the taunt. The billionaire studied him, curious, as if he were a bug rather than a human who was minutes away from losing everything.

Fuck it.

Griff shoved the rest of his chips into the center of the table. The stack toppled with a clatter. "I'm all in."

It was reckless, considering his hand, but Grant was right. There was no point in delaying the inevitable slaughter. He fanned out his cards, a tiny spark of hope flickering in his chest.

There was still a chance. It was one of the things he loved about poker. Those moments when you misread your opponent, and the luck still breaks your way. Griff had certainly had worse hands...

But then Grant fanned out his own cards, grinning.

Griff didn't need to look to know he'd lost, but he did anyway, clocking the straight. He felt bile in the back of his throat and swallowed the bitterness. Wasn't that just the way? The rich just get richer.

"Well, that's a real shame, isn't it?" Grant said, chuckling as he lifted a finger to Katia for another scotch. "I mean, you went to all that trouble just to fail. I almost hate to see it happen."

Griff felt sick, but he wasn't going to give the man the pleasure of knowing it. Despite the heavy weight of exhaustion, he had plans to make. There was no way he was leaving Rue with this asshole, no matter what he'd promised. There were some things more important than honor.

Griff forced himself to look in Grant's smug face, leaned back in his chair as if he hadn't just lost. He was in no position to make demands, but he made one anyway. "I want to see Rue before I go."

Over Grant's shoulder, Katia winced.

***

At the ripe age of twenty-four, there were two things Sarah knew she was bad at: staying sober and following her uptight brother's arbitrary rules, which is probably how she found herself flying across the Pacific in a stolen jet.

Griff had told her to stay put and take care of the dogs, but she wasn't in the habit of listening to authority. Or following the rules. Plus, her stupid, arrogant brother needed *her* help for once. It was an opportunity she couldn't pass up.

"I really shouldn't be doing this," Benji complained for the tenth time since they'd left the runway. He'd been standing beside the squat concrete building at Grant's little airfield, getting a Snickers from the vending machine, when she pulled into the abandoned gravel driveway. To his credit, he'd only sworn and shaken his head before trudging back to the jet.

Now, he fiddled with a knob overhead, tapped on a random gauge, and took another sip of coffee from a battered Starbucks tumbler. Sarah rolled her eyes, propping her bare feet on either side of some important-looking buttons on the dashboard.

"You make a point of following the rules, Benny?" she asked, already knowing the truth. One of the rare superpowers of being a fuck-up was being able to spot fuck-up-ery in other people.

Benji the pilot was cute in a rumpled college-dropout sort of way, especially once he was out of that stuffy pilot uniform, but his unshaven face and wrinkled Blink 182 T-shirt didn't exactly scream success. His aw-shucks smile must have gotten him laid plenty of times, but it wouldn't work on her. She'd dated one too many sorry cases in her life, and she wasn't about to add another notch to that belt.

Benji grumbled something unflattering and then said, "A pilot is required to be off twelve hours out of every twenty-four according to the FAA, and this is already my third ocean crossing in two days!"

Sarah was an expert at taking risks and making terrible decisions, but she didn't have a death wish. She'd let Benji nap for a few hours in the back of the plane before making him gear up for another hop over to Hawaii.

He'd been surprisingly willing after seeing the pics she'd taken with his family dog, a 14-year-old Golden named Buttons. The gun hadn't even been loaded. She felt kinda bad about manipulating him with fake violence, but she couldn't stomach a six-hour flight in economy even if she did have the money to blow on a family rescue mission. So poor Benji it was.

His finger tapped restlessly on the throttle, but as far as she could tell, he'd barely touched the controls since they reached cruising altitude. He had a twitchiness to him that she recognized all too well. Thank god for autopilot.

"Benny, did you take an upper before we took off?" she asked, feigning innocence.

Benji's finger stopped tapping. His eyes slid over to hers, filled with guilt. Something passed between them—the sort of understanding that could only be found between two people who'd leaned on something unsavory to get them through this dumpster fire of a life. Trouble recognized trouble.

"Maybe stop being a pain in my ass, or I'll report you to the FAA," she said, yawning and wiggling her toes. She definitely wasn't going to do that. She was a lot of things, but a snitch was not one of them.

Luckily, good ol' Benny didn't know that. He scowled and turned back to the windshield, patting Turnip's head absently. Sarah tried not to be charmed, but it was hard to be mad at a man flying a plane with a giant potato on his lap.

Turnip wiggled in his sleep, slobbering on Benji's jeans, tongue lolling out. The pilot huffed in fake annoyance and patted the dog's belly. It made a satisfying hollow thump.

Tug was there too, squeezed between their seats in the tiny cockpit, even though the whole plane was available behind him. His giant head rested on some important-looking plane stuff in the center console. Sarah wasn't sure when she'd become a dogsitter, but she'd had worse jobs.

"Were you really going to kill my parents?" Benji asked as they sailed through the clouds. His hair stuck up around his headgear like straw. She wondered if he was a gamer. She had a special place in her heart for gamers.

"Wouldn't you like to know?" she teased.

Benji was looking less and less convinced of her potential for danger, which was probably a bad sign given their location in the middle of the ocean. She should probably try to be more imposing, but she just didn't have the heart to be scary anymore. He glanced over at her, his gaze lingering a little too long on her bare legs.

She'd changed into cutoffs and a t-shirt as soon as they left the continental United States, more than ready to be somewhere warm and very, very far from home.

"What's your plan?" Benji asked, " Once we get there?"

"Wouldn't you like to know?" she repeated, giving him a sassy wink. The truth was, she had no idea. Plans weren't really her thing.

It was Benji's turn to roll his eyes.

They were silent for a minute, the cockpit filled with the lulling hum of the engine and Turnip's light snores. Dappled sunlight filtered through the windshield, dancing around the cockpit. The chairs were surprisingly comfortable. Sarah briefly considered dozing, wondering if she would wake to find Benny had turned them back toward—

"I have a place," Benji announced, pushing some buttons when the jet wavered slightly. "On the island."

Sarah looked over, surprised, but Benji's eyes were still on the horizon. One hand rested loosely on the throttle, the other balancing his coffee cup on his knee. He looked like he was in the driver's seat of a Honda Civic instead of a million-dollar jet.

She couldn't help but notice that he had a nice profile, a boyish face with full lips and long eyelashes.

"You have a place?" she repeated, wondering where this was going. "Just casually? On one of the most expensive islands in the world?"

He shrugged sheepishly. "Don't get excited. It was my grandparents, and they haven't renovated since the 70s. Just a little two-bedroom shack on the North side of the island."

Her last apartment had been a duplex she'd shared with three other losers and a komodo dragon named Stanley. It had been a shit hole that smelled like mildew and lizard and shared a wall with an angry couple that needed therapy.

"Must be nice," she said.

Benny raised an eyebrow. His eyes were the exact shade of the sky behind him. "Don't pretend your brother isn't rolling in it."

This was true, but she'd never considered Griff's money to be hers. Maybe that was part of the problem.

"What I'm saying," he continued, taking another sip of his coffee. "If you'd stop being such a little bitch—is that you can use the house as a home base."

The offer startled a laugh out of her. "Are you trying to get in my pants, Benny?"

This time, when he looked over, his gaze wasn't subtle. He wiggled his eyebrows and grinned. "Maybe."

Twenty-Six

Rue wasn't sure how many miles she had walked. Her legs ached from sinking in the sugar-white sand, but it was hard to complain because on one side, the ocean undulated between deep blue and sparkling turquoise, and on the other, the green mountains sprouted straight up from the beach, their peaks teasing wispy clouds.

As soon as she'd left Grant's manicured property, the shoreline had become more rugged and wild. The beach was littered with coconut shells and fallen palms. Craggy patches of grass pocked the sand in some places, and in others, old lava flows broke up the stretches of clean beach with jagged black rock. Those she scrambled over, grateful for her stolen sneakers, pausing occasionally to watch the colorful fish dart through the pockets of tide water.

She stopped to swim once, stripping down to her underwear to wash off the sweat, sand, and fear, before setting off again, too afraid of being spotted to linger long. At some point, the beach started to hug the road that circled the island. It was mostly empty, but Rue ended up hiding in the shadows of palms at every flash of headlights. There was no knowing when Grant would discover she was missing, but she was certain he'd send Benson out to hunt her down.

Even if she didn't have a death wish, hitchhiking was out of the question. She wouldn't be safe until she reached civilization. So she kept walking.

Eventually, she passed a few houses, far more modest than Grant's monstrous estate, but locked and abandoned. Probably vacation rentals. She had briefly considered breaking into one, but adding burglar to her list of problems didn't seem wise.

She had just started to look for a place to stop for the evening when a dune buggy appeared on the beach in the distance. Even from far away, she could tell it was one of those four-seaters with huge off-roading wheels, sand spraying behind it. There was no reason to believe it was for her, but she stopped anyway, watching it bump over the uneven sand.

Rue lifted a hand to shade her eyes. A girl was standing in the passenger seat, clinging to the roll bar, and waving vigorously. Rue glanced over her shoulder to confirm that David Hasselhoff wasn't running behind her, Baywatch style, and then squinted again at the approaching vehicle.

The waving woman was young and wearing cutoffs and a tank top. Her hair was bleached blonde and cut into a bob. She was grinning like someone who'd just won a game show. She waved wildly again, and this time, Rue lifted a hand in recognition.

Sarah.

It took her brain a second to compute that Griff's little sister was about to rescue her from an empty beach on an island in the middle of the ocean. The last time she'd seen Sarah, the girl had been snuggled up with Tug in Griff's house, looking miserable.

The dune buggy bumped over the last small dune, spraying sand dramatically before coming to a stop a few feet away. Rue didn't recognize the driver. Cute, with a backwards ball cap and a baby face, he didn't seem like a threat. A plastic purple lei hung around his neck.

"Aloha!" Sarah chirped, still clinging to the roll bar. "Fancy meeting you here!"

Rue limped over. Her skin was sandblasted from the wind, and she suspected a nasty sunburn was forming on her shoulders. There was a blister on her left heel.

"Sarah?"

Griff's sister grinned. A pair of plastic yellow sunglasses held back her windblown hair, the price tag still dangling from one arm. She waved at the back seats where a blue IGLOO cooler already occupied half of the space.

"I'm here to rescue you! Well, *we* are. This is Benny—Grant's pilot. Get in!"

Rue hesitated at the name Grant, but Sarah seemed to trust him, and she was out of options, so she got in, sinking into the dune buggy seat with a sigh.

"Benny?" she asked.

The driver looked over his shoulder and attempted to scowl, although it wasn't very effective on his boy-next-door face. "Benji. I've been kidnapped."

"Seems to be going around," she joked, but her voice was drowned out by the engine revving back to life.

Sarah playfully slapped Benji on the shoulder and sat back down, propping her feet on the dash. Rue admired the girl's ability to flirt even in the middle of a dangerous getaway.

Neither of them asked her any questions as they lurched into motion. It was a rough ride and loud. Rue gripped the edge of the seat, stomach flipping, and wondered when this day from hell would be over.

"Where's Griff?" she yelled, flipping open the cooler beside her. It was mostly filled with beer.

"These two," Rue muttered to herself. Thankfully, there were also a bottle of water, condensation still dripping along the sides, and some sort of rice patty wrapped in seaweed. Grateful, she pulled them both out.

Sarah turned, one hand on poor Benji's shoulder as they bounced along. Her hair whipped in her face, and her eyes sparkled. "Rescuing you, of course!"

***

There was no reason for Grant to let him see Rue, other than to gloat, but the billionaire gallantly led him through the estate, commenting on the decor as if he were a realtor instead of the asshole who'd just fleeced him.

Griff followed him up the grand staircase and past an obnoxious marble bust of Grant's face before stopping in front of an enormous mahogany door, one of many in the long hallway. The doorknob was a bronze peacock. It was as ostentatious as it was beautiful.

It had only taken a couple of hours to transfer all his assets into Grant's name. Only a handful of phone calls to sign over his home, the BMW, and the money in his bank accounts. It didn't seem like enough time to ruin a man's life.

Grant graciously let him keep a few thousand dollars and the deed to the truck. Griff wasn't stupid enough not to be grateful, and he hated that most of all.

Katia stood outside the bedroom door, her face pinched, delicate hands clasped tightly in front of her. She stepped forward to unlock the bedroom, and then wobbled on her high heels, before catching herself with a grimace. Griff barely looked at her. There were more important things to think about—like how to crush Rue's heart.

The door opened. Griff half expected Rue to launch herself into his arms, but the bedroom was quiet and dark. Grant swept a hand forward, no doubt marveling at his own graciousness. "I'll give you a moment of privacy to explain the situation to our...friend. Perhaps that will help expedite her cooperation."

"Fuck you," Griff responded and stepped inside, closing the door behind him.

Moonlight spilled through the balcony doors. It was dark and quiet. Rue must be sleeping, exhausted from being dragged halfway across the globe. It was a beautiful prison, at least. The white canopy rustled around the bed frame, and the air was perfumed with salt and orange blossoms.

Griff tried to ignore the hole in his stomach as he ducked underneath the canopy. The bed covers were in a shambles, the white duvet spilling over one side, pillows askew. It was also empty.

"Rue?" he called, lifting his voice just above a whisper. His heart thudded as he cocked his head, listening, but the only sound was the ocean. He crouched to look under the bed. There was only dust, and her discarded pajamas crumbled in a ball.

Griff flicked on the lamp beside the bed, half expecting to find Rue hiding in a shadow with a vase raised above her head, but the room was empty, and a quick search of the bathroom only revealed a damp towel that smelled like her.

He stepped onto the balcony, ignoring the sound of Katia rapping on the door, as he peered over the railing. It was a long drop, and the ground below was undisturbed. There were no clues as to where she had gone. Not a scrap of fabric or stand of dark hair caught in the railing, but there *was* a second balcony three feet away.

And a narrow ledge.

Twenty-Seven

"Took you long enough," Sarah said, squinting up at him from where she was sprawled in a lounge chair. A pair of plastic yellow sunglasses was perched on top of her head. Her nose was already starting to sunburn.

It had taken him all morning (minus a stop for an acai bowl and bullet coffee) to track her to Benji's shitty rental property on the North side of the island. Benji was asleep in the chair next to her, an ALOHA ball cap tilted to cover his face, his hairless chest still streaked with sunscreen. Condensation from the beer in his hand dripped over his knuckles. It was 10 am.

Neither of them had answered his knocks, but the front door had been open anyway. Benji's house was small and hadn't been renovated since the 70's. The couch in the living room was brown and gold with worn armrests, and the glimpse he'd gotten of the living room revealed an avocado colored refrigerator and a matching stove. However, the entire back wall was made up of long glass doors that folded open to reveal a million-dollar view of the ocean.

It was nothing compared to Grant's lavish mansion, but it was charming and comfortable and probably worth more than most people could afford in a lifetime.

Benji and Sarah had dragged loungers into the middle of the back lawn. A gentle breeze kicked off the waves, which crashed a dozen yards past a crumbling brick seawall, but it was still brutally hot. Tug was sprawled in the dappled shade of a palm, his pink toes stretched out in the grass.

There was no sign of Turnip. Or Rue.

"Sarah, what the hell?" Griff said, rubbing the back of his neck to keep from strangling her. He was desperately in need of a shower, and the sight of these two knuckleheads sunbathing filled him with unhinged rage.

Sarah was wearing a purple bikini underneath a wet t-shirt, but Benji must have gone swimming in his khaki shorts. Griff couldn't help but notice that his own morning hadn't involved a lovely dip in the ocean.

Sarah raised an eyebrow at his tone, but then flicked her sunglasses over her eyes and went back to her tanning. "You can't be mad—I saved your magical girlfriend."

Griff opened his mouth to ask why she wasn't back in Oregon with the dogs and then shut it again. Her reckless decision to get involved had saved his ass this time. Not to mention Rue's. He couldn't honestly remember a time when *Sarah* had saved *him*. It had been the other way around since she was caught shoplifting lipstick from CVS in 6th grade.

Griff sat down on the seawall beside her, hands dangling between his knees. It wasn't comfortable. The brick had been eaten away by salt and time, exposing the white mortar, which dug into his ass, but he was too tired to figure out something else.

From his new angle, he could see the faint rainbow that arched above the house's roof and the surfers taking advantage of a swell a ways down the beach. It was hard to stay mad in paradise.

Sarah rubbed her shin with the back of her heel. "My phone died on the plane, and I forgot to pick up a charging cord at the ABC."

But you remembered beer, Griff thought, not that he was surprised. It was a classic Sarah move.

Griff wanted to ask about Rue. She was here somewhere. He'd seen the sandy sneakers kicked off by the entryway, too small for Sarah's big ass feet.

He needed to apologize. To explain how he was going to make it right. Except he didn't know how to do either of those things.

He was thinking about asking for one of those cold beers after all, when Turnip appeared, trundling over to him slowly, stubby tail wagging. Amused, Griff watched until the dog head butted him in the shin before hefting him into his lap.

"Thanks," Griff grumbled, as Turnip squirmed on his back, exposing his belly for pets. Griff rolled his eyes and obliged.

Sarah lifted her head off the lounge chair, cupping one hand to her ear. "What was that?"

He scowled. "You heard me."

She shrugged and pulled a tube of sunscreen from underneath her thigh. Benji was still snoring. A cheap purple lei dangled from his neck, and there was a suspiciously large pile of Hawaiian snacks sitting at the end of the lounger. Griff wondered if they'd robbed the ABC.

"She's pretty pissed at you," Sarah said mildly, smearing sunscreen on her cheeks.

He was not interested in discussing his love life with his sister. "Where is she?"

Sarah pointed down the beach. "Went for a swim."

A dozen more small houses dotted the shoreline, but the beach itself was empty. In the near distance, the shoreline curved out of view, but a few people still surfed the reef. Fuck, he didn't want to do this.

He stood anyway. He was a lot of things, but coward wasn't one of them.

"Griff?" Sarah was sitting up now, her legs crossed in front of her. "Are you going to be okay?"

The collar of her t-shirt had fallen off one shoulder, and the sun had already given her skin a soft glow. She looked better. Despite everything he'd fucked up, Sarah looked better. Griff's heart lifted.

"I'm always okay." It was the kind of answer you gave to worried sisters. The kind that was also a lie.

She snagged his wrist when he turned to go. Her hands were still slippery from the sunscreen, and she smelled like a damn pina colada, but there was something in her eyes that made him pause.

"She's a good one," she said.

The sun was relentless on the crown of his head, as if hell itself were punishing him. His lips twisted. He thought of the way Rue's hips moved while she cooked and the sparkle in her eyes when she laughed.

"I know."

Sarah squinted up at him, head tilted. There was something innocent about her. A hopefulness still hidden inside her that only time would steal. He envied it.

"Don't fuck this up," she said softly.

He grimaced and pulled away. "I already have."

***

"Your brother's got a real kidnapping problem, huh?" Benji asked, taking a sip of warm beer. Sarah propped her head up with one arm, watching Griff disappear down the beach. Her forehead and the tops of her knees were starting to burn, but the sun felt too good to move to the shade.

"He tries too hard. Even when we were kids, he always had to be on the winning team," she said, shaking her head at the memory. "It wasn't enough to play soccer just because it was fun. He had to get the trophy. Had to be on the honor roll. God, I remember him crying the time he got a B on his report card. Heaven forbid something in his life be less than perfect."

Like her.

She'd been a straight C student. The only time she'd won any-thing had been the time she sold the most Girl Scout cookies in the county, and that had only been because her mom had taken the order sheet to work. Some people were born winners. Which meant that others were born, well, losers.

She couldn't be fixed. It was something she'd accepted a long time ago.

Benji rolled over to look at her. He was fair, and the sun had burned across his nose, bringing out the faintest smattering of freckles. He was built like someone who used to work out, his muscles soft but still defined. It was nice to look at.

"Most people stop short of committing crimes to get what they want," he said.

Sarah sighed, annoyed at her instinct to defend her tight-ass brother. "Yeah, well, Griff likes a challenge."

Benji hummed noncommittally, his gaze skimming brazenly over her bare legs. "What about you?"

He had turned his hat backwards, and it made him look even more like a college frat boy than normal. His eyes were the same blue as the sky behind him.

"I excel at committing crimes," she teased.

Benji grinned. "I gathered that. What else?"

Sarah felt herself squirm inside. Most guys were fine with a flirty non-answer, happy to move on from the what-is-your-relation-ship-to-your-parents to the playful banter. She was much more comfortable when men just wanted to fuck her.

"What were you like as a kid?" Benji probed, taking another drink.

"A kid?" she said, stalling.

Most people assumed they knew her type—toxic family life leads to a descent into drugs and partying—as if her whole life was a story they'd already read. These days, everyone was obsessed with where she was going, rather than where she'd been.

Benji held his hand three feet above the grass, demonstrating a child's height. "Yeah, kids. You know those slightly smaller adults?"

She glared at him. "I know what kids are, Benny."

Benji rolled back onto his back, putting an arm underneath his head. He was still wearing the plastic lei, and the sparse smattering of chest hair caught the sunlight. Sarah tried not to notice the way it trailed down his stomach.

"I wanted to be an astronaut," he told the sky. "I went on a field trip to the Air and Space Museum in D.C. when I was six, and it was like I entered a damn cult. By second grade, I knew the names of every astronaut who ever lived. In order of when they went to space, of course. My bedroom walls were plastered with posters of jets and rockets. My parents got so sick of buying me toy planes for Christmas that they tried to convince me to take up video games just for something new."

Sarah laughed, imagining a little Benny surrounded by his beloved planes, and then quickly sobered. Sure, he was a fuck up, but at least he'd done something with his life. At least he'd stepped on the path.

"I like fish," she blurted, fiddling with her sunglasses.

Benji turned his head, shading his eyes with his hand. "Fish?"

She shrugged, embarrassed. "I thought I might be a marine biologist. I wasn't obsessed like you, but I feel most like myself near the ocean. I won a goldfish at the fair once. My mom let me keep him in a small bowl, but then I saved my allowance to get a bubbler and plants...His name was Puppy." She gave him a side glance. "I really wanted a dog."

Benji laughed.

It had been a long time since she'd thought about Puppy, but she could still imagine his little body swimming around the glowing tank. She would watch him while she fell asleep, listening to the aquarium engine hum. There was something comforting about the orange glint of his tiny scales and the steady flutter of his gills as he swam around and around his tiny kingdom.

"He lived eight years, which is ancient for a goldfish," Sarah said wistfully. "It was the only time anyone trusted me to keep anything alive."

As a teenager, she'd never been asked to babysit or pet sit, or even house sit. Not so much as keeping an eye on the neighbor kid or watering a plant. She swallowed and tried to smile, but Benji didn't smile back. He reached between the loungers and touched the back of her hand.

It was barely a touch, but she knew what it meant. This was the moment before he leaned across to kiss her. The moment before the sex and the laughter and the leaving. She was glad to be back on familiar ground, but then Benji withdrew his hand.

Confused, she watched him look at the ocean and then back to her before he asked, "Have you ever been snorkeling?"

Snorkeling? She'd never been out of Oregon.

She shook her head, thinking of all the YouTube videos she'd watched of people gliding through crystal water and darting fish. Thought of all the times she'd imagined jumping off sailboats and swimming through colorful reefs. It had seemed so far away, but now...

Benji nodded, as if deciding something, and sat up. "Let's go!"

Twenty-Eight

Rue straddled the surfboard and studied the waves on the horizon. The ocean swelled rhythmically underneath her, matching the slow beat of her heart. A school of silver fish darted underneath the board, brushing her feet and occasionally nipping at her toes. She didn't bother shaking them off. For a moment, she was part of it—the waves and the squinting blue sky and the slow sea turtle riding the current toward the reef. It was the only time she felt part of something, really.

Rue flicked her wet hair over her shoulder, squinting through salt-stung eyes at the incoming set. Underneath her palm, the surface of the long board she'd found in Benji's shed was rough with old wax and a little big for her, but it did the job.

She'd lost track of how long she'd been surfing, but her sunscreen was definitely starting to fail. Her shoulders burned, and her sternum was raw from surfer's rash. She'd gashed her shin on a coral outcrop a while ago, and it throbbed in time with her heart. She never felt better.

It had been so long since she surfed anything other than the frigid, rough waters off the west coast that she'd almost forgotten what it was like to catch a glassy wave on a warm, sunny day. She wasn't the only one. A dozen surfers were tackling the break a little further out, but she was out of practice and preferred the calmer waves closer to shore.

Rue picked out her next wave, swung the board around, and started to paddle. The swell bloomed beneath her, and she popped to her feet, feeling the familiar rush when her balance steadied. The wave curled behind her. She pumped, skimming her fingertips along the inside of it, laughing when it spat her out the other side.

She gave in to gravity and tipped off the board into the swirling white water. It tumbled her like a washing machine, but she stayed calm, holding her breath until her head broke free. She gasped for breath, finding her footing while the board tugged at the leash around her ankle like an impatient puppy. She laughed, blinking salt from her eyes, and grabbed for the board. Maybe one more—

Griff was standing on the beach beside her towel.

Rue pushed her wet hair from her face, aware she must look like she just finished wrestling a shark. Her chest heaved, and she could feel the adrenaline burning across her cheeks.

Griff, on the other hand, looked handsome and entirely out of place even from a distance, like a romantic lead who'd gotten lost on his way to somewhere much more important than her. His hands were deep in the pockets of his rumpled trousers, and he was barefoot, the ocean soaking the cuffs. His white dress shirt was unbuttoned, flapping around his trim waist. His hair was disheveled in just the right way, flickering in the ocean breeze.

She couldn't quite see his eyes, but she could feel them on her, dark and intense.

Rue forced herself not to adjust her bathing suit. Sarah had bought it for her at one of those beach stores that sold boogie boards and oversized t-shirts. The suit was sapphire blue and way too skimpy for surfing, but the color looked surprisingly nice against her pale skin, although it did nothing to hide the rolls at her hips or the jiggle of her thighs.

Rue was surprised to find she didn't care. She felt too good to hate herself, so she decided not to.

Griff saw her looking and lifted a hand. Rue gathered the board, mentally bracing herself as she splashed over to him. "Fancy meeting you here."

Up close, the illusion of the romantic lead faded quickly. Griff's hair looked like it could use a wash, and there was darkness beneath his eyes. He looked miserable.

"Why didn't you tell me you surfed?" he asked, hands still buried in his pockets, brow furrowed.

She shrugged, clutching the board awkwardly against her hip. "You didn't ask."

"I'm an asshole."

Rue wrinkled her nose. "Unfortunately, that is true."

Griff didn't laugh, shaking his head ruefully. "I fucked everything up, Rue."

This was true. She didn't exactly know what had happened while she was escaping Grant's estate, but she had a good guess. "Everything?"

He waved a helpless hand. "I shouldn't have...this all started out so...I wouldn't blame you if you never..."

Griff's shirt fluttered around his waist. There was a smattering of freckles hidden in his chest hair that she hadn't noticed before, and he needed a belt. His pants rode dangerously low.

Rue tried not to be distracted by his hip bones. She was mad at him. Furious, in fact. But it was hard to remember why with the sun drying the salt on her skin.

"You're terrible at this," she heard herself say. "Apologizing."

His eyes flicked up to hers at the teasing tone, as if he'd expected fire and brimstone. The sliver of hope in them made her stomach flip-flop.

"I'm still mad," she insisted, shifting the board. Her arms already ached from holding it.

Griff nodded, squinting out at the ocean.

"So what happened, exactly? At Grant's?" she asked, bending to undo the surf leash.

"I could ask you the same thing," he responded, taking the board from her as soon as she was unlatched, ignoring the way the ocean soaked into his pants. She plucked her towel off the sand, wrapping it around her shoulders. Rue knew a stall when she heard one, but she relented, telling him about the plane ride and the balcony and the dune buggy rescue as they headed back toward Benji's.

Griff chuckled when she came to the part about Katia and Grant's mistress. "You're....something else, Rue Adler."

She would have been offended if it hadn't sounded so much like a compliment. "Your turn."

"I lost." He looked at the ocean when he said it, face grim.

Rue raised her eyebrow. Suddenly, the slump of his shoulders and the haunted eyes made sense. He wasn't the kind of person who was used to losing.

Luckily, she was.

"What was the bet?" she asked, scrubbing at her hair with the towel as Benji's came into view.

"Everything."

She stopped in her tracks. "And by everything you mean..."

His eyes slid away from hers. "You. The house. My fucking investments. You know, everything."

Rue frowned, tring to understand. "You bet everything you owned on one card game to...save me?"

He held up his hands, empty palms flashing. "I'm so, SO sorry. I know you're not an object—or something to be won at a damn poker table. I just wasn't sure how else to *fix* things, and then I lost, and you had escaped anyway! Just...fuck."

She licked her lips, tasting the brine. "You did this because of my Luck?"

"What? No. I did it so you could escape this fucking mess I got you into."

The sun was warm and steady on the crown of her head as she stared at him, trying to take in this new information. His dirty hair fell over his eyes, and he muttered angrily to himself, holding the long board easily against his side. His shirt was soaked and he was covered in sand.

Griff had traded his whole life for her. A near stranger. A one-night stand. For her—not her Luck.

Twenty-Nine

Rue was bleeding. Griff stared at the cut on her shin instead of her eyes, the blood washing away with each incoming wave. Bits of sand glinted like fairy dust in her dark hair, and her belly pillowed softly over her ridiculous neon blue bikini. She had a surf rash on her sternum, the skin red and raw where the board wax had scraped. Griff had never seen anything more beautiful.

When he finally looked up, her bottle-green eyes were searching his face, the towel forgotten in her hand. It was hard to hold her gaze, but he forced himself to anyway. Griff couldn't tell by her expression if the apology was working, but at least she wasn't telling him to fuck off. She must have been surfing for a while because her cheeks were pink from the sun, and adorable patches of sand and tiny shells were stuck to her skin.

He liked her so damn much.

He wanted to surf with her in every ocean. Wanted to kneel in front of her in the warm sand and lick the salt from her skin. Wanted to lie on sweaty, twisted sheets in the darkness and listen to her talk and talk. Wanted to play cards on a Friday night with zero stakes, except to make her laugh. He wanted to foster a thousand dogs together.

And he'd thrown it all away for a little extra Luck. He was a spectacularly stupid man.

"Carry my towel?" Rue asked. Her tone was gentle, which made no sense since he just told her that he'd wagered her like a piece of meat in a poker game AND LOST. But he wasn't stupid. He knew an olive branch when it slapped him in the face.

Griff stepped closer and took the soggy towel. She smelled like salt and sweat and suntan lotion. He didn't want to step away, but he did, flicking the wet towel over his shoulder. He didn't deserve to be close to her.

Rue started walking again, close enough that their shoulders brushed, and he followed. The crashing ocean filled the awkward silence.

"I'm sorry," Griff said again, because there was nothing left to say.

Rue nodded and made a circling gesture with her finger. "More."

Griff thought he saw a hint of a smile. Fair enough.

"I was a dick," he said, his feet sinking in the wet sand. "I should have trusted that you could handle yourself because you are a competent, amazing, beautiful woman. I am a terrible hero. Terrible."

"More."

This time, she was definitely smiling. His heart leapt. "You're not a bargaining chip. Or a good luck charm. And I am an asshole for thinking you were for even one second."

They'd made it to Benji's house. Rue paused at the bottom of the sea walls' crumbling steps. There was no one outside except for a couple of gulls watching them from the worn bricks. The lawn chairs were empty.

Griff rested the nose of the board in the sand, waiting.

"I forgive you," she said simply, her eyes soft.

Griff blinked, sure he'd heard wrong. "You do?"

A breeze had kicked up, lifting the edges of her hair. Sand glittered in her wet eyelashes. She was a damn surf goddess. "Yes."

He swallowed, wondering if her Luck might be working after all. "Um, may I ask why?"

She shrugged. "You lost everything. I have nothing. Seems like a great place to start."

His head swirled. It must be the sun or the lack of sleep, but he was pretty sure he was misunderstanding this conversation. "Start?"

She smiled again, crossing her arms in a way that pushed her breasts up. Yes, he was definitely losing the thread of the conversation. He squinted at her, trying to keep his gaze off the softness of her wet skin.

"Griff?"

"Hm?"

"I could use a shower."

***

The house was, indeed, blessedly empty. A bottle of sunscreen lay on the grass between the two lounge chairs, but Sarah and Benji had made themselves scarce. Griff made a mental note to thank his sister as he followed Rue across the lawn. Griff spotted a note fluttering on the dining room table inside, pinned with a sweating can of Dr Pepper, but he didn't bother going inside to read it. There were more important things to focus on—like watching Rue bend over to rinse her board with the hose.

The palm trees created dappled patterns of sunlight across her back. The strings of her suit dug into her hips, creating cute rolls as she splashed water on her feet, swiping at the blood on her shin with one hand. She looked sweaty and sunburned and impossibly sexy.

Griff shrugged off his ruined shirt, flinging it over one of the chairs along with her towel. Rue had said that cryptic thing about the shower, but he wasn't going to assume she wanted him to join her—although he *really* wanted to assume. Wanted to assume the fuck out of it.

"I don't think you're going to get clean that way," he said, as she tried to clean her sandy legs with equally sandy hands. Her blue bikini bottoms had twisted in the back to expose one ass cheek. His palms itched.

Rue straightened, one hand on her luscious hip. She lifted an eyebrow in his direction and looked him up and down. "You could use a shower yourself."

She was right. He smelled like airplane and panic.

For some reason, though, hot and sweaty looked good on Rue. A drop of sweat slid down her neck before dipping into the hollow of her throat. He forced himself not to follow the path it made as it continued over her chest and between her perfect—

Rue stepped close and wrapped her arms around his neck as if hugging were something they did every day. Startled, his hands ended up politely on her upper back, which was the stupidest place to be when ass and hips existed. Her suit was shockingly cold against his bare chest, green eyes luminous as she peered up at him.

"What are you going to do now?" she asked softly. Her gaze dipped to his lips as if she wanted to watch his answer.

"Right now? At this very second?" he asked, voice strangled. If that was the question, he had some thoughts.

Rue brushed her lips lightly against his before pulling back again. It was barely a kiss, but it was like licking an electric wire, the spark waking every part of him. She tasted like salt. Like a long day on the board. Like a margarita rim.

"What are you going to do with your new life as a poor man?" she replied, smiling. Her fingers teased the hair on the back of his neck. He tried to focus on her words, but his hands slipped from their polite location to rest on the small of her back.

"Be with you," he said impulsively.

She slipped one naked leg between his, gently pressing against his hardness with her thigh. He'd never been so damn turned on without actually being inside a girl.

"Right now? At this very second?" she whispered, leaning forward to kiss his neck.

His hand found her jaw. He tilted her face up to his. "I want to be with you, for-fucking-ever if possible."

Her pulse raced beneath his fingers. Her green eyes were luminous. There was hope there, but also doubt. Doubt he'd put there. Doubt he was planning on obliterating one promise at a time.

She kissed him again, but this time he was ready, catching her smile and pulling her closer. He explored her lips thoroughly before finding her neck, tasting the salt and bitterness from the sunscreen. He couldn't give a fuck. He wanted to taste every inch of her. Wanted to kneel down and pull aside her ridiculous blue bikini and lick inside...

"Shower," Rue gasped, stepping away from him so suddenly he stumbled. She put a hand on his arm to steady him.

Right. They were still on the lawn.

Truthfully, he didn't care if they were rolling around on a public beach as long as he could be with her, inside her, above her, but she caught his hand and pulled him toward the side of the house.

Griff changed his mind about the public beach when he saw the outdoor shower on the side of Benji's house. It was enclosed in graying teak slats and covered in blooming plumeria vines. The sweet scent of the white flowers perfumed the air. Two brightly colored beach towels were draped over the swinging door.

He followed Rue inside. The shower head was one of those fancy waterfall kinds, and the wood floor underneath their feet was surprisingly spider-free. Griff was reassessing Benji's life choices when Rue pulled off her top, dropping it behind her with a wet plop.

Griff stopped thinking about Benji.

Her nipples pebbled despite the heat. He could already taste them, salty and cold between his lips.

There was just one thing.

"Rue?"

She tilted her head, looking suddenly shy. "Griff?"

"Are you sure about this? About us?"

For one breathtakingly long second, she was still, thinking. Griff was just starting to curse his own mind-blowing stupidity when she stepped close, standing on her tiptoes to kiss him.

She took his hand and guided it between her legs. "Why don't you find out?"

He should say more, advocate for dumping him at the very least, but instead, his finger slipped past the fabric of her skimpy bikini and inside her slick heat. She whimpered.

Griff reached around her and turned on the shower. They both gasped at the first splash of cold water, clutching each other until it became warm rain. He kissed her, sipping the water from her lips and the dip of her collarbone before pushing her gently against the shower wall. Water cascaded over her shoulders, droplets catching on her nipples and dipping into her belly button.

He knelt, ignoring his ruined pants, and kissed her soft thigh.

"Griff," she sighed, her fingers in his hair.

He took his time, his breath hot between her legs before moving aside the damp suit to lick into her heat. This time when she said his name, it was not a sigh.

He could have moved fast, then. Could have flicked his tongue and made her knees buckle, but instead, he lapped slowly, tasting the ocean between her thighs. Rue trembled and squirmed above him as he worked, but far too soon, her first orgasm took her.

He was content to stay kneeling in front of her until she fully melted, but the third time she said his name, it was a demand, so he stood, blinking water from his eyes.

Rue's hands were at his waist, fumbling with his fly, trying to free him from his soggy pants. He could have helped, but he let her struggle for a minute, his whole body vibrating as her knuckles brushed against his hardness.

"Fuck," she swore, finally, laughing. It was the best sound he'd ever heard.

He chuckled and helped, shucking the last of his clothes and stepping into her until there was no room for the shower water between them. They clung to each other for a moment, but her body was slick and wet against his, and he couldn't wait any longer. Didn't want to wait.

He spun her around, forcing her to brace her hands against the shower wall. Water cascaded down the arch of her spine, sipping past a faded tattoo on her shoulder and slicing her ass cheeks. He kissed the back of her neck, shoved aside her bikini, and plunged inside her.

She almost bucked him off, but he caught her, one hand stretched across her belly as he settled inside her. Shower sex wasn't always the best, but she was slick and hot, and somehow it worked.

Griff bent his head, nearly drowning under the shower's onslaught as she wiggled against him. He kissed her shoulder blades and began to move, setting a brutal rhythm. She writhed underneath him, begging with her body, until he couldn't wait any longer and gave her what she wanted until they were both shuddering under the hot Hawaiian sun.

Later, he would tuck Rue against his chest as Benji tended the bonfire on the beach. They would watch the glowing embers spark and disappear into the night sky, as the driftwood popped and spit. His sister would be there, the low murmur of her laugh mingling with the hush-rush of the tide while she flirted with the smiling pilot. They'd pass plastic containers of poke with chopsticks sticking from the top and watch the moon rise.

Later, Rue would be there, her hair tickling his cheek, smelling of salt and sea and his future. It was magic, one way or the other, and which he didn't so much care anymore.

Thirty

EPILOGUE

"Remember that sometimes not getting what you want is a wonderful stroke of luck."—Dali Lama XIV

The sky above the canyon was the color of a bruise, the sun still trapped just below the jagged rim, but the rising heat was already burning off the dew that clung to the dry grass. A dry wind swept up the gorge, rustling Rue's hair. She pushed the strands from her eyes and secured the worn bandana as the campfire sparked to life between her boots.

She didn't know exactly where they were because there was no service out here in the middle of nowhere, but she guessed somewhere in Arizona from the red dust that coated everything. She'd kill for a hot shower. Would commit crimes for a steaming latte from her angry gay barista. Would kidnap someone's mother for a soft mattress. She'd never been happier.

Behind her, Tug sniffed around the wheels of their RV, searching for the perfect spot for his morning constitutional. She'd left Griff snoring on the cramped bed inside, half the mattress taken up by Turnip's limp body. Her back ached just thinking about it. Rue balanced a dented pot of water on top of the sputtering fire and decided that tonight might be a motel night.

They'd been on the road (the run?) for six months.

After much discussion, Griff had reluctantly left Sarah at Benji's small, tropical paradise and flown back to the mainland. They'd managed to scrape together enough money from Rue's meager savings and Griff's remaining money to buy a used RV that they hooked up to his old truck. She wasn't sure Grant was a threat anymore, but neither one of them wanted to find out.

Rue got regular texts from Addie, showing off the shelter's cutest new residents and complaining about colleagues. It was the only thing she really missed.

The sunrises made up for it, though.

Below them in the canyon, the river murmured, its white rapids swollen from the spring rains. Occasionally, a hawk screeched across the gorge on the way to a nest hidden in the steep walls. She'd never breathed such clean air.

Rue carefully took the pot off the fire and poured the boiling water into the French press she'd prepared the night before. The smell of coffee mingled with wood smoke as she waited for it to steep. It was a far cry from Griff's fancy espresso machine.

After three minutes, she poured a cup into a speckled blue tin mug and watched the sun breach the horizon. Streaks of light turning everything to gold. The small canyon wasn't famous to anyone but the stray kayaker enjoying the raging river below. It wasn't a famous national park or roadside attraction. No one posted selfies in front of it on Instagram.

Rue could still hear the highway traffic a mile away. Their camping spot was just a patch of red dirt and a hastily made fire ring. It might have been the most beautiful place she'd ever seen if they hadn't driven through Montana, explored Highway 1 on the Pacific Coast, or hiked the green mountains in Maui.

Behind her, the RV door squeaked open. Rue smiled without turning and reached for a second mug, pouring the coffee as Griff flopped next to her on the log they'd dragged next to the fire last night.

"I can't believe we have this place all to ourselves," Griff said, scratching his cheek and yawning as he stretched out his legs. He was in desperate need of a shave, but she secretly loved the scruffy look.

"Must be luck," she said, leaning over to kiss his scratchy cheek.

He grinned and elbowed her good-naturedly. "At least you're useful for something, cause it's not driving the rig."

"You said I wouldn't have to drive that thing!" she protested, glaring over her shoulder at the RV.

"Yeah, yeah, whatever."

Griff winked at her, looking deliciously rumpled. He'd thrown a ratty old flannel over his sweats and shoved his feet into dirty Crocs. He smelled like campfire and grease. She loved him.

Rue rested her head on his shoulder, squinting into the rising sun. "How's Sarah?"

She felt him shrug. The siblings had been FaceTiming when she fell asleep last night, so she'd missed the end of the conversation.

"She's kinda freaking out about her Bio class, but she's gotten an online tutor that I think will help. Benji seems to think she's doing fine academically and is just overthinking it."

"What do you think?" Rue asked as Turnip finally ambled down the RV steps and plopped down on her feet. She gave him a scratch between the ears.

"I think I've never seen her care so much about anything before."

Rue nuzzled into his neck. Griff turned and found her lips. He tasted like coffee.

"I'm so glad she's okay," she murmured.

He smiled into her hair. "Me too."

They sat for a while, watching the sky fade from pink to blue. Eventually, Griff got up to make breakfast, frying two eggs in leftover bacon grease while she toasted a few slices of bread against a hot rock. They ate slowly, with a second cup of strong coffee. It was the last of the food, unless you counted Dorito crumbs and half of a stale chocolate muffin she'd picked up at the last gas station.

It was time to move on.

"Where to next?" Rue asked, munching on the burnt corner of a slice of bacon.

Griff glanced sideways at her, his empty plate still balanced on his knee. "How about home?"

She looked at him, admiring how soft his smoky eyes had become since they ran away. How easy his laughs came. She didn't care anymore, if it was luck or love that had brought them together, just that they were. Together.

"We don't have a home," she said, thinking about her dream to open her own shelter. Thinking about holidays with Sarah and Benji and a small, cozy home filled with love.

"You wanna make one?" Griff asked, quietly.

Rue smiled.

She did. She really did.

ACKnOWLeDGements

I couldn't follow my dream of becoming an author without the support of my husband, Joel. He helped me edit this little rom-com despite being a lover of sci-fi and space operas. Thanks for hitching your ride to an artist.

Noel, I wouldn't be a writer without you. You make me a better person and a better writer. I'm grateful you exist.

To my kids, Caden and Taro, for being proud of who I am outside of being your mom. You're the best cheerleaders. I love you both so much.

My love of reading started with laps and libraries. It started with snuggles at bedtime and drifting off to the voice of someone reading Good Night, Moon or The Four-Story Mistake for the hundredth time. Thank you to my Mom and Dad for being those voices.

Finally, I am grateful to all my readers, especially my family, for their support over the years.

ABOUT THE AUTHOR

Rebecca Barto is a former library kid, still trying to survive with hoodies, headphones, and tattered paperbacks. After years as an elementary teacher and a professional chef—careers that taught her how to balance heart, patience, and precision—she found her true she finally found her passion in writing.

Her previous works include *Silverfish*, a YA Appalachian ghost story, and *Between Light and Night*, a dystopian fantasy. No matter the genre, Rebecca strives to weave magic into every story. She lives in Asheville, NC, with her husband and two very good dogs.

www.ingramcontent.com/pod-product-compliance
Lightning Source LLC
Chambersburg PA
CBHW051942220626
47052CB00004B/757